Longarm stood at the corner of a building, as planned, and waited. When he stepped into Willy's path, the thug was moving so fast he plowed into Longarm. They both went flying. Now Willy was winded and badly scraped up. Longarm tackled him in the middle of an intersection.

"You're under arrest!" he shouted into Willy's face. But Willy pulled his knife and stabbed at Longarm, slicing his pants at the knee. Longarm jumped back and growled, "You're just determined to send yourself to prison for a long while, aren't you?"

"Go to hell, Marshal Long! I wasn't doin' nothin' wrong. You feds are just out to get me."

"At least you got part of that right," Longarm said. "Now drop the knife, Willy. I don't want to have to shoot you." Willy's eyes were bugged and glazed with something other than alcohol. Maybe he'd been to the opium den.

Longarm was wearing his Colt on his left hip, butt forward. But before he could pull his gun, Willy leapt at him, knife slashing. Willy was incredibly fast, even if he was high. Longarm took a vicious slice across the forearm and then backhanded Willy in the mouth so hard that the man's head rocked on his shoulders and his lips gushed with blood. Wild with rage, Willy staggered and attacked again. Longarm had no choice now but to pull out his Colt revolver . . .

TABOR EVANS

LONGARM

AND THE MISSING MISTRESS

JOVE BOOKS, NEW YORK

THE BERKLEY PUBLISHING GROUP
Published by the Penguin Group
Penguin Group (USA) Inc.
375 Hudson Street, New York, New York 10014, USA

Penguin Group (Canada), 90 Eglinton Avenue East, Suite 700, Toronto, Ontario M4P 2Y3, Canada
(a division of Pearson Penguin Canada Inc.)
Penguin Books Ltd., 80 Strand, London WC2R 0RL, England
Penguin Group Ireland, 25 St. Stephen's Green, Dublin 2, Ireland (a division of Penguin Books Ltd.)
Penguin Group (Australia), 250 Camberwell Road, Camberwell, Victoria 3124, Australia
(a division of Pearson Australia Group Pty. Ltd.)
Penguin Books India Pvt. Ltd., 11 Community Centre, Panchsheel Park, New Delhi—110 017, India
Penguin Group (NZ), Cnr. Airborne and Rosedale Roads, Albany, Auckland 1310, New Zealand
(a division of Pearson New Zealand Ltd.)
Penguin Books (South Africa) (Pty.) Ltd., 24 Sturdee Avenue, Rosebank, Johannesburg 2196,
South Africa

Penguin Books Ltd., Registered Offices: 80 Strand, London WC2R 0RL, England

This is a work of fiction. Names, characters, places, and incidents either are the product of the author's imagination or are used fictitiously, and any resemblance to actual persons, living or dead, business establishments, events, or locales is entirely coincidental.

LONGARM AND THE MISSING MISTRESS

A Jove Book / published by arrangement with the author

PRINTING HISTORY
Jove edition / September 2005

ISBN: 0-515-14011-2

JOVE®
Jove Books are published by The Berkley Publishing Group,
a division of Penguin Group (USA) Inc.,
375 Hudson Street, New York, New York 10014.
JOVE is a registered trademark of Penguin Group (USA) Inc.
The "J" design is a trademark belonging to Penguin Group (USA) Inc.

PRINTED IN THE UNITED STATES OF AMERICA

10 9 8 7 6 5 4 3 2 1

Chapter 1

It was a hot Colorado day in July when Deputy United States Marshal Custis Long picked up the newspaper and read that Miss Lilly Claire was going to be singing at Denver's Birdcage Theater for a special week's engagement.

"She's probably the most beautiful woman in America," Deputy Marshal Jed Connor observed. "What I wouldn't give to have that woman in my arms for just one hour!"

Jed was a greenhorn when it came to both women and being a lawman. He was barely in his twenties, but he couldn't be faulted for his exuberance. Longarm especially was amused because young Jed Connor seemed to fall in love at the mere sight of a beautiful woman. In time, the newly appointed marshal would learn that many beautiful women were schemers out to break a man's heart or take all his money, but until then, Longarm would enjoy the young marshal's innocence.

Longarm studied the picture of the famous singer. Lilly Claire had lots of curls framing a heart-shaped face and he had to admit that she was quite the beauty. Still, if only to get his friend's goat, he shrugged and said, "Well, Jed, I guess she's all right."

"All right!" Conner exclaimed. "The woman is an angel! She's fantastic! Have you ever seen her perform on stage?"

"No." Longarm glanced up Colfax Avenue suddenly spotting a dangerous pickpocket and thug that regularly frequented the downtown area. "The truth is, Jed, that I'm not much of a theatergoer. I'd rather be a participant than a spectator in most everything I do."

"Well," Connor said. "If you ever laid eyes on Miss Claire, you'd change your mind about that in one helluva hurry!"

"Look down the street," Longarm said, "but don't be too obvious."

Jed glanced up the avenue. "Who is that guy?"

"Willy Pike. I haven't seen him working this area in over two weeks," Longarm said, "but that's because he knows we're looking to arrest him."

"For picking pockets?"

"Assault and battery," Longarm said. "Willy approached a rich old man here on Colfax Avenue about two weeks ago. Normally, he'd have picked the man clean, but Willy got greedy. He dragged the gentleman into an alley and knocked him senseless before robbing him of his watch and jewelry."

"That's right," Jed said, suddenly remembering. "Didn't the old man die from that assault?"

"No. He was expected to die, but he pulled through. Willy got lucky on that one, but if he's moved up to assaulting his victims, we need to take him off the streets right now."

"You know that I'm always game," Jed answered. "How do you want to play this?"

"Willy knows me on sight," Longarm said. "So you

stay right here and pretend to be reading your newspaper. I'll circle around the block. When you go for Willy, he's streetwise enough to know you're the law and he'll rabbit. I'll be waiting for him down the street."

"Is Willy armed?"

"Probably," Longarm said. "I know he always carries a knife and he's not afraid to use it."

"Then be careful when I flush him your way."

"I will," Longarm vowed. "Willy doesn't look too impressive under that big coat. But he's strong and he's quick. I consider the man very dangerous and he won't give up when he's collared."

"I'll back you up," Jed promised. "Don't worry about that, Custis."

"It never entered my mind that you wouldn't. Can you run?"

"I'm not the fastest man in town, that's for sure."

"Well," Longarm said, "do your best to make a match of it. If Willy is pressed hard, he won't be looking ahead for anyone in ambush."

"All right," Jed promised, taking a few deep breaths. "Signal me down the block when you're in position."

"Right," Longarm told the young deputy as he started off.

It only took Longarm a few minutes to get into position. Then, he raised his hand in signal and Jed moved toward the felon. And sure enough, it didn't take Willy but a few seconds to realize that he had been spotted by the law. He wore a sailor's knit cap tight over his head and Willy was a tall, lanky character who could run like a deer when flushed.

"Hey!" Jed shouted as he broke into a run after the fugitive. "Stop!"

Willy made a very uncomplimentary gesture toward

the young deputy, then took off at a dead run. Longarm stood at the corner of a building and waited. He saw Willy knock a young couple to the sidewalk and then bowl a lovely lady over as if she were a mannequin. The lady went sprawling into the street, then jumped up and shouted an oath at Willy who began to laugh as his long legs increased the distance between himself and Deputy Marshal Conner, who wasn't at all fast on his feet.

Willy was still laughing when Longarm stepped into the thug's path. The wanted man was moving so fast that he didn't have time to think so he instinctively lowered his head and plowed into Longarm. They both went flying. When Longarm regained his feet, Willy was up and running again. But now the man was winded and badly scraped up by his collision and tumble on the sidewalk. He was also limping. Longarm, being a tall, athletic man, closed the gap and tackled Willy in the middle of an intersection.

"You're under arrest!" Longarm shouted into Willy's face. "Don't make matters any worse than they already are."

But either Willy wasn't listening or else he didn't give a damn. In either event, he pulled his knife and stabbed at Longarm, slicing his pants at the knee. That made Longarm even angrier since the pants were almost new. He jumped back and growled, "Willy, you're just bound and determined to send yourself to prison for a long while, aren't you?"

"Go to hell, Marshal Long! I wasn't doin' nothin' wrong. You federal assholes are just out to get me."

"At least you got part of that right," Longarm said. "Now drop the knife, Willy. I don't want to have to shoot you."

"Not a chance." Willy's eyes were bugged and glazed with something other than alcohol. Maybe he'd been to an opium den. Longarm couldn't be sure, but he saw that Willy was flushed and acting crazy.

4

Longarm was wearing his Colt on his left hip, butt forward. "I guess we'll have to do this the hard way."

But before he could pull his gun, Willy leapt at him, knife slashing. Willy was incredibly fast, even if he was high on drugs. Longarm took a vicious slice across the forearm and then backhanded Willy in the mouth so hard that the man's head rocked on his shoulders and his lips gushed with blood.

Wild with rage Willy staggered and attacked again. Longarm had no choice now but to pull his Colt revolver and shoot Willy dead center in the chest. The pickpocket turned mugger dropped his knife and lifted up on the toes of his worn shoes. He stared down at the widening stain on his chest and then cried, "Marshal, dammit, you just shot me dead!"

"Afraid so."

"Well, damn you to hell!"

Longarm knew the man was finished and he felt bad that things had turned out this deadly. "I warned you to drop the knife, Willy. I tried to get you to do this the easy way but you wouldn't listen."

Willy took a faltering step backward and then he collapsed to the sidewalk cursing with bloody red bubbles foaming on his thin lips.

Longarm knelt and searched Willy. He found a derringer and several wallets that the man had just lifted from an unsuspecting citizen. "So long, Willy. You're going to hell."

Willy gagged out a curse and died.

Marshal Jed Connor arrived out of breath and panting like a fire horse. "You shot him dead?"

"I had no choice," Longarm said, raising his forearm to show Jed his injury. "Willy was high on something stronger than whiskey. He must have gotten into some bad opium at a chinaman's den."

"How bad are you hurt?" Jed asked.

"Not bad, but I'll probably need some stitches."

"Damn! I wish I was a faster runner."

"That's all right," Longarm said. "It's done. Willy was crazy and it's best that he's no longer among us."

"I agree!"

Longarm raised his head to see none other than Miss Lilly Claire approaching. She was scuffed and her elbow was bloody. "Miss, you must be the woman that Willy knocked down back there on the street."

"That's right," Lilly said. "And the one who yelled out that cuss word that probably shocked half of Denver. Marshal, are you all right?"

"I'm going to be fine," Longarm told her as a crowd gathered to stare at the dead man. "But I wish this had turned out differently."

"I don't," Lilly said. "The man was a killer. Congratulations for your bravery."

"I was trying to help, too," Jed stammered, pulling off his hat and wringing it like a towel. "We're both federal officers of the law. But I'm the one who is a great fan of yours, Miss Claire."

"Thank you," she said, eyes never leaving Longarm. "Marshal, I'd like to find some way to repay you for your dedication to duty and extreme bravery."

"It goes with the job," Longarm told her.

"Sir," she said, turning to Jed. "I saw that you are not much of a runner, but would you please run and find a doctor?"

Jed was crushed. "I . . . I . . . sure. I'll be right back, Miss Claire. And don't worry about me."

"Why should I? You weren't the one who had to stop that crazy man and be hurt in the process."

"Yes, ma'am."

Jed trotted off and Longarm felt sorry for the young deputy. He clearly idolized Miss Claire and would have loved to be in her company.

"Marshal, please remove your jacket and let me see what I can do with that wound until the doctor arrives."

"It's nothing. Just a scratch."

"*A scratch*? Why, Marshal, you're bleeding all over the sidewalk."

Longarm looked and saw that he was making a mess. Not nearly as much as Willy, of course, but a mess all the same. He shrugged out of his coat and let the famous singer roll up his bloody shirtsleeve.

"This is a very nasty cut," Lilly said, taking a silk handkerchief from her purse and tying it over the wound. "You'll definitely need some stitches."

"I expect so."

"Marshal," she said, when the wound was at least covered and the bleeding somewhat staunched. "I'd really like to repay you for your bravery. If only with an invitation to come and hear me sing tonight. A front row seat for you."

"I appreciate that," Longarm said, "but my young friend Jed is your real fan."

"Then bring him along and I'll have two front row seats waiting. And afterward, perhaps you could join me in my sitting room for a glass of champagne."

"What for?"

"To celebrate the fact that you're alive and that thug is dead," Lilly said as if it should have been obvious. "And so, will you promise to come and bring your slow-footed young friend?"

"I sure will," Longarm said, not wanting to appear rude.

"Good." Lilly kissed Longarm on the cheek. "Are all of the federal officers in Denver as dashing and handsome as you?"

7

Longarm didn't have a reply. Maybe none was even expected. Lilly looked down at Willy's body, gave it a kick in the side and then turned on her high heels and marched back down the street.

"Why did she do that?" a gentleman asked, looking shocked.

"You mean kick Willy?"

"Yes. That was a terrible thing to do to a dead man."

Longarm shrugged. "Willy ran her over. Didn't you see the scrape on her arm?"

"Sure, but the man is dead."

"Then he didn't feel the kick in the ribs," Longarm said. "Now all you folks just go about your business. Go on. Spectacle is over. Move along."

Longarm turned to see Miss Lilly Claire being helped into a very fine coach by a tall, dark and handsome man. For just a moment, the famous lady looked his way and their eyes met. Then, she entered the coach and was whisked away.

Jed arrived with a doctor in tow. "Custis, are you all right?"

He felt a little embarrassed. "Just a scratch on the arm, Jed. Doc, I should have found you. Not the other way around."

"That's all right," the man said, opening his medical kit. "Let's see that nasty wound."

While the doctor unwrapped the bloody silk handkerchief that Lilly had given him, Longarm said, "Couldn't you just tape it up tight, Doc? No need to make a fuss 'cause it'll heal up just fine."

The doctor was in his fifties. Short and plump with a take-charge air about him. "Twelve stitches at the least," he announced. "Come along. Follow me to my office."

Longarm, grumbling because he didn't like to go to the

doctor and have stitches, turned to follow the short man.

"Hey," Jed asked. "What about Willy's body?"

"Send for a mortician and write up a report and give it to the boss," Longarm called back over his shoulder.

"Okay!" Jed said, looking disappointed. "Oh, Custis?"

"Yeah?"

"Did Miss Claire present you with that pink handkerchief?"

The bloody rag was lying on the sidewalk. "Yep."

"Can I keep it?"

Longarm shook his head. He couldn't, for the life of him, imagine why any man would want to keep a ruined pink handkerchief. But Jed clearly wanted the thing so Longarm yelled, "Sure, Jed. Now get down to business."

The young deputy marshal beamed while Longarm followed the doctor just hating the idea of getting a dozen damned stitches.

Chapter 2

Longarm really didn't want to go to the Birdcage Theater that night to see Miss Claire sing, but a promise was a promise. And besides, Jed was pounding on his door and excited to go. So, more not to disappoint his lovesick friend than to see Lilly sing, Longarm consented to attend the theater.

"How's that arm feeling?" Jed asked as they made their way toward the Birdcage with hot air still rising from the city sidewalks.

Longarm was in a foul mood. "It feels a lot worse since the doctor put in all those stitches. I should have ditched the man and just doctored it up on my own. If you bind a wound like that and keep it clean it will knit together just fine on its own accord."

"Yeah, but it would leave a much wider scar."

"What do I care about scars?" Longarm asked, feeling ill used. "I got 'em all over my body."

"So I've heard," Jed remarked. "They say in the office that you've been shot no less than five times."

"That's about right."

"And stabbed a dozen."

"I wouldn't argue with that," Longarm told his young friend.

"Well, I sure don't want to end up like you," Jed told him with a solemn shake of his head. "Not that I'm afraid to get hurt . . . but nobody wants to be a walking scar."

"That's a poor way of describing me," Longarm groused before coming to a stop. "Here's the Shamrock Pub. A bit of old Ireland. Let's go in and have a drink or two before we get to the Birdcage."

"But Custis! Miss Lilly comes on in an hour!"

"Well," Longarm told his friend, "if you want to sit in a hot, stuffy theater for an hour waiting, go on ahead. I'm going to stop in for a couple of drinks. Make both my arm and my disposition a lot better."

"All right," Jed agreed. "I'll go in with you . . . but only for one quick whiskey and then we've got to be on our way. The theater will be packed and we sure don't want to miss out on those front row seats."

"No," Longarm said without trying to hide his sarcasm, "we sure wouldn't want to do that."

Longarm went into the Shamrock and felt better almost immediately. The inside of the pub was cool and filled with festive Irishmen, most of whom were drinking dark Irish beers or whiskey.

"Two whiskeys," Longarm called to the bartender he knew well. "And Michael, better make 'em doubles. We're in for a long evening."

Their whiskey was called Murphy's Milk and it was imported from Dublin. To Longarm, it was one of the strongest but smoothest whiskeys available even though it cost far more than the usual swill.

"To the late pickpocket turned mugger known as Willy Pike," Longarm said, raising his glass in a grave toast. "He

12

wasn't much of a man on this earth, maybe he'll be a better one in the next world."

"To Willy," Jed agreed, as they tossed their drinks down.

"Bartender, bring us another round," Longarm called, as he felt the whiskey roll smoothly down into the base of his belly.

"Strong stuff," Jed said in a hoarse voice. "But good."

"Murphy's Milk is the best," Longarm told the young deputy. "It'll stand you up straight and it won't treat you bad in the morning like cheap whiskey and beer."

"To you," Jed said, making the second toast.

"Naw," Longarm countered, "to Miss Lilly Claire."

Jed nodded enthusiastically. "I'll drink to that!"

After that second round, they sort of forgot about time. Even so, they would have gotten to the Birdcage Theater for the opening soon except for the mean brawl that erupted between a couple of Irishmen. One of them was a big, hump-shouldered fellow who looked as if he could knock down a draft horse with one punch. The other fellow was slender, but quicker with his fists and more than game. Longarm didn't know what the fight was about, nor did he care to interrupt the fracas, except that the bigger man got the smaller one down and started kicking him in the head.

"Hey!" Longarm shouted. "Stop that or you'll kill him. You won the fight so step back and be done with it!"

The big man wasn't ready to quit fighting. "He called me mother a rotten whore!"

"Is she?" Jed asked, not realizing this was the wrong thing to ask.

The big man's eyes blazed and he charged the young deputy marshal, grabbed him around the chest in a bear hug and lifted Jed right off the ground. Then, he butted Jed

13

twice in the face, breaking the young deputy's nose. Longarm saw Jed's eyes roll up in his head.

"Turn him loose," Longarm ordered. "My young friend meant no insult to your mother."

"Is that right?" the huge Irishman said, dropping Jed like a sack of potatoes. "And how do *you* know that to be true?"

"Because he doesn't even know your mother," Longarm answered. "And, if he did, Jed would probably know that she *is* a whore. So there's no insult, really, just a truth."

The big Irishman was having a little trouble following Longarm's line of reasoning, but he eventually decided that Longarm had also insulted his mother.

"You'll be apologizing for those foul words!"

Longarm wasn't in any mood to apologize. Not this evening. And besides, he wasn't happy about Jed Connor getting his nose broken. Now the young deputy marshal would need to be taken to a doctor.

"Well," Longarm said to the angry Irishman, "I guess you've messed up two men here tonight. Want to try to do it to a third?"

"You bein' him?"

"I bein' him," Longarm said, managing a cold smile.

The Irishman lunged at Longarm with outstretched arms no doubt planning to also get him in a terrible bear hug and then bang his nose into a bloody pulp. Longarm stopped that plan with a wicked uppercut to the Irishman's solar plexus, right below where his ribs met at the sternum. The blow had all of Longarm's strength and weight behind it and it stopped the big man's bull rush. The Irishman's cheeks blew out and his face turned as pale as the belly of a fish. His mouth flew open and he tried to suck wind but Longarm hit him again, only this time with an overhand left that broke the man's crooked nose.

The Irish rounder howled but it wasn't out of pain as much as rage. He took a couple of steps back, set himself and then charged with both fists flying. Longarm dodged the attack and dug a hard right into the man's kidneys as he passed. The Irish brawler collided with the bar and clung to it for a moment, half dazed. Longarm shot a left cross to the man's ear that spun him completely around.

"Damn you!" the Irishman hissed, trying to grab Longarm. "I'll tear your head off!"

Longarm stepped back and waited to see if the man was going to come at him one more time.

"You've probably had enough."

"I ain't begun to fight!" the Irishman bellowed as he staggered toward Longarm with his fists up but his eyes glazed.

Longarm ducked a roundhouse punch that would have knocked a wall down. He came up from a crouch and slammed a right uppercut into the Irishman's lantern jaw. The man's head snapped back and Longarm stuck a stiff left jab into the big man's Adam's apple.

The Irishman's eyes bugged and he choked, grabbing his throat and fighting for air once again.

Longarm hoped that he had not hit the man so hard in the throat that he would choke to death. He watched his opponent sit down hard on the sawdust floor, his face turning purple.

"You might have killed him!" Jed cried with blood streaming down his face.

"That wasn't my intention," Longarm said, hurrying over to the Irishman and grabbing the man's wild red hair. He pulled the Irishman's head down on his chest and pounded on his back a few times. He'd done this before and it seemed to help and this time was no different. At last, the Irishman was able to breathe and Longarm even helped the man to his feet.

"Bartender," he said, "buy this fella a beer on me."

"Yes, sir!"

"Look at my nose!" Jed cried. "It's broken!"

"They always heal."

"But I can't go to the Birdcage to see Miss Claire looking like this!"

"Oh, well," Longarm said with a shrug of his broad shoulders. "We all share a few of life's disappointments. Let's just pass on the theater tonight."

Jed was devastated. "You can't do that to a famous lady like Miss Lilly Claire!"

"Sure I can. There will be hundreds of adoring fans cheering her on at the Birdcage. She won't miss us even a little."

And with that, he grabbed Jed and helped him out of the Shamrock Pub asking, "Do you even know how to fight?"

"Sure!" Jed said defensively.

"Well, from what I just saw, you aren't much good at it."

Jed said something that was unintelligible.

"Speak up plain!" Longarm ordered.

"I said you have to go see Miss Lilly!" Jed cried, cupping his bloody nose with both hands.

"Why?"

"Because you promised you would!"

Longarm gave the matter some thought. Then, he pulled out his Ingersol railroad watch, the one that had a hideout derringer attached to the watch chain. "The show has just started. It's too late."

"Please!" Jed cried. "Tell her that I wanted to come but had an . . . an accident."

Longarm could see that this meant the world to his young friend. He was also starting to think that Jed Connor really wasn't tough, quick-thinking or resourceful enough to make it as a deputy United States marshal.

"Look, Jed. I'll go hear the woman sing if you'll find a doctor and have him reset that nose. If you don't do it this evening, it will be a lot harder to do in the morning . . . and far more painful."

"All right. I'll do it."

"Then I'll go see Miss Lilly Claire sing," Longarm promised. "And I'll tell you all about it."

Jed was devastated more by missing Miss Lilly's performance than he was by his injury. "Damn my luck for getting my nose broken!"

"Luck didn't have much to do with it," Longarm told the man. "Jed, you really must learn to duck."

"I'll try to remember that," Jed promised as he lowered his head and walked away.

Miss Lilly Claire was well into her performance when Longarm came down the aisle and found the two empty front row seats. He took one and leaned back in his chair and made himself smile. Miss Lilly, as he should have expected, did not even appear to notice that he had arrived late. Most of the crowd were men and everyone was making liberal use of their personal flasks of whiskey. All in all, it was a rowdy, well-oiled crowd.

Lilly was singing a song called, "Baby Blue Eyes." It was a stupid song about a lover with beautiful, but love-crossed blue eyes. Or maybe the boyfriend was cross-eyed. Either way, Longarm didn't much care.

17

Despite its stupid lyrics and the poor piano accompaniment, Longarm soon realized that Miss Lilly really did have an exceptionally fine voice and stage presence. She was a vixen and temptress enough to make her audience pant with pure lust. Miss Lilly wore a skimpy black silk dress adorned with red ostrich feathers. When the feathers waved with her energetic movements, they gave the crowd the impression that Lilly Claire was baring her beautiful bosom. And there was also plenty of shapely leg to admire. Lilly wore black knit stockings and the hem of her dress was so high that you could see her garters whenever she made a high kick step.

The crowd loved her performance, and Lilly Claire got a steady round of applause and wolf whistles. Song after stupid song, she was as much an actress as a singer and when she finished, "Pearl the Little Orphan Girl," there was not a dry eye in the whole theater . . . except for Longarm's amused brown ones.

The performance ran until ten o'clock and the crowd kept calling Miss Lilly back for an encore. When she finally left the stage for good, Longarm got up and followed the admiring crowd out the door. He was tired and his arm still hurt because of the dozen stitches. Even more troubling was that he now saw that the arm had bled again and ruined the sleeve of his favorite dress coat.

"Marshal?"

Longarm turned to see the handsome man he'd observed helping Lilly into her coach. "Yes?"

"Miss Claire would like to see you in her dressing room right now."

"Look," he began, "it's late and I'm not . . ."

"It is not nice to disappoint Miss Claire." The man had an imperious air that Longarm did not like. He added, "Please follow me."

Despite the word *please* Longarm had a notion to ignore the request, but he'd never been to a theater dressing room. Besides, he was curious about the woman and knew that Jed Connor would be thrilled to have a little information about someone he obviously worshiped.

"You were late," Lilly said when Longarm was ushered into her huge and plush dressing room. "And you have blood on your clothes and face."

He raised his sleeve. "I must have pulled a couple of fresh stitches free by accident."

"And scraped your knuckles on a bar top, I suppose?" she asked. "You look, quite frankly, like you've been in another fight."

Longarm chose silence.

"How did you enjoy my performance tonight?"

"You have a fine voice," he told her. "And a great connection with a male audience."

"That's the only kind of audience I'll play to," she answered. "Because women don't seem to appreciate my . . . talent nearly so much."

"Not surprising," he said. "Women can be jealous in the face of unusual beauty."

Her eyes widened. They were gray and large. "What a nice compliment! And I was just beginning to think I'd made a mistake by inviting you to my private dressing room."

"Who's the guy who led me here?"

"Would you believe it if I told you that his name is Edward and he's my half brother?"

"No, I wouldn't believe that."

Lilly's eyes widened with surprise, and then she laughed. "You are very frank and very, very dangerous. I can see that and it excites me."

"Excites you?" Longarm didn't understand.

"Yes. Dangerous men have always excited me. I detest

boring men and you are certainly not one of those. Would you like some champagne?"

"Is it *good* champagne?" he asked. "Because I've drank cheap champagne and it always gives me a splitting headache the next morning."

"With all of your fighting, I wouldn't think that a hangover would be of any consequence to a big and hard man such as yourself, Marshal."

"You'd be wrong."

She laughed. "I only drink French champagne. The very best."

"Then I'll have some."

Lilly did nothing more than clap her hands twice and her "half brother" Edward appeared. She ordered him to bring a bottle and two glasses. Longarm could not help but notice that he looked angry and humiliated. But he did what Lilly ordered.

"To you, Marshal Long," she said, giving him a bold look.

"And to you as well," he offered, wondering what . . . if anything . . . would happen when they finished the excellent French champagne.

Chapter 3

"Well, Marshal, what is your full name?" Lilly asked as she refilled their glasses with the bubbly. "Or are you sort of the strong and mysterious type who prefers action and no talk?"

Longarm was resting on a very nice, soft sofa. He smiled and shook his head. "I'm not at all mysterious, Miss Claire."

"Lilly," she told him. "Let's not be formal with each other. I invited you here for a reason."

"Which I've been wondering about," he said.

Lilly gave him a decidedly wicked smile and managed, without being obvious, to hike her dress up several inches so that he could see most of her lovely thighs. "I'll just bet you have."

Longarm could not help but feel a stirring in his pants despite the pain in his forearm, and the combined effects of whiskey and champagne. "I'm waiting to hear it, Lilly."

"I have a proposition for you."

"Good."

"I want you to be my *new* personal protector."

"You mean bodyguard?"

"That's right."

"Not interested."

"I will double whatever you're earning as a federal marshal."

"Still not interested," he told her. "I like my job and do it well."

She frowned. "Let me be more specific. I am under a death threat here in Denver. I need someone who is brave and resourceful and tough to keep me alive during my current engagement at the Birdcage Theater."

"So you just need someone to watch over you for a week?"

"That's right," Lilly said. "But, if you are up to snuff, I'd offer you permanent employment."

"Thanks," he said, taking a swallow, "but that's not my line of work. I'm a deputy United States marshal, and I like my job just fine. Being another Edward, like that poor fella out there, doesn't appeal to me in the least."

Lilly emptied her glass and wiggled her shoulders so that her large breasts, still wreathed in red ostrich feathers, moved provocatively. "Does *five hundred dollars* for seven days of very easy work appeal to you, Marshal?"

Longarm couldn't help but smile. "Is that all you'd pay . . . or would there be some other . . . ah, benefits to go with the job?"

She licked her lips and her gray eyes dropped to the small tent that was forming in his pants. "I think that there would be other very, very special rewards besides the money."

Lilly thought she had him by the gonads, but Longarm never had been a fool over women. He loved them and even respected and admired most of them, but he had never been dangled on any woman's string. Not like poor Deputy Marshal Jed Connor who would have attempted back flips for such a generous and intriguing offer from this sensuous singer.

"Lilly," he said, rising to his feet and emptying his glass. "I've had a rough day and I'm not quite up to par tonight. I want to thank you for the excellent French champagne. . . . I've never drank its equal. But . . ."

"*One thousand dollars* for seven days, Marshal. And you get whatever you want from me in the way of pure carnal pleasure."

The offer was so abrupt and startling that Longarm sat back down again. "Are you serious?"

"Deadly serious," she answered. "My life is in the gravest peril. And I need your help."

"Who is it that wants to kill you and why?"

"I don't know his name. But I do know he is crazy in love with me and that he is here in Denver. I have notes from him."

"Threatening murder?" Longarm asked.

"Yes, if I don't engage in his wild sexual fantasies starting tonight."

"Why don't you take the notes to the police and ask for their protection?"

Lilly drained her glass and refilled. "Because he has sworn that if he sees a policeman near me, he will not only ambush the policeman with a high-powered hunting rifle, but he will also shoot me dead."

Longarm frowned. "Maybe you should just leave Denver."

"And maybe he will follow me wherever I go," Lilly snapped. "In fact, he implies as much. Custis, I need to end this nightmare and I need to do it very soon. I don't want to die and I don't want a policeman to die."

"But you don't mind if I die?"

She laughed, but there was no humor. "In the first place, you don't wear a uniform. In the second place, I believe you are clever and skilled enough to protect me against this crazy stalker."

"What about Edward?"

Again, she laughed without humor. "Edward really is my half brother. And he is protective, but unskilled. He carries a revolver and a knife, but admits he couldn't hit the broad side of a barn with a shotgun. I don't want him in the way of a bullet. He would just . . . botch things up and make them worse."

"That's not too flattering an assessment of your half brother."

"Edward has many skills," Lilly said. "And he is loyal and dedicated to my welfare. I pay him well, of course, but he goes beyond that. He is reckless, hot-headed and well meaning, but he would only make this deadly matter worse."

"Does he even know of these notes and threats?"

"Of course. And he is very much opposed to my offering you this temporary and possibly permanent job."

"I image he's jealous."

Lilly sighed. "If that is true, it is only because he is afraid that you might replace him. It's nothing more than that, I promise."

Longarm leaned back on the sofa and considered this woman. "A thousand dollars for seven days?"

"If you catch the man who is writing those terrible

notes," Lilly said evenly. "If you merely deflect him, then I'll pay you five hundred. Still, that's about what . . . six months of your normal wages?"

"Close enough," Longarm said. "I suppose I could take a week off from my job. I have a lot of unused vacation time due me."

"Then do we have a deal?" she asked, setting her empty glass on a table and removing the red ostrich feathers.

Longarm couldn't help but gape. Lilly's breasts were not only large, but perfectly formed. Giant and succulent peaches.

"Why don't we seal this arrangement by doing something that will end your day on a high note?" Lilly asked, beginning to undress.

Longarm was not a fool over women, but neither was he a fool enough to turn down what was being offered.

"I'll talk to my boss first thing tomorrow morning," he said with a grin as she quickly undressed and showed him the rest of her lush landscape. "I'm sure that he will understand."

"Yes," she said, coming to him and unbuttoning his gunbelt, then his trousers. "I'm sure that, if he is a reasonable man, he will understand."

Moments later, Lilly was on the couch wearing only a huge, seductive smile. Longarm stood next to her while she stroked his massive rod and then sucked on it with delight.

"Do you know how to use this, Marshal Custis Long?" she purred, licking the head of his shaft with her pink tongue.

"I've been told that I do not often disappoint," he said thickly.

"I'll just bet you have," Lilly whispered as he climbed

between her lovely white thighs and buried himself deep in her wet heat.

Longarm took Miss Lilly slow and easy. He played her as skillfully as she played him and it probably lasted a half hour, maybe more before they both lost control of themselves and began to plunge and thrust in mindless passion.

"Lilly!" Edward called from outside. "Are you all right in there?"

"Fine!" she trilled. "Oh, *so* fine!"

Edward tried to open the door but Lilly had been wise enough to lock it earlier. "Lilly!"

"Go away!" she cried, wrapping her legs around Longarm and squeezing the last of his seed into her sweet wetness. "Edward, dammit, get lost!"

Longarm heard the man curse, then stomp away.

"I think he hates me now even more than he might have before."

"Edward is harmless," she cooed, rocking back and forth to milk the last bit of pleasure from their coupling. "But I will have him bring another bottle of champagne. Ours is almost empty."

"It's as empty as I am now."

"Yes," she cooed, "but that will soon change, won't it, Custis?"

"Oh, yeah," he growled, rolling off her and feeling as big and strong as a horse.

"Your poor arm. It's bleeding again!"

"Who cares?" Longarm asked. "There is a lot more where it came from."

She reached out and grabbed his manhood. And with a dead serious tone said, "There had better be."

Longarm wasn't worried. He would get the seven days off and he'd more than satisfy this black-haired beauty's sexual appetite. And the other thing was that he had every intention of finding out who wanted to kill Miss Lilly Claire so that he could not only protect her, but earn that thousand dollars.

Chapter 4

"You're what?" Marshal Billy Vail roared.

"I'm taking a week off to do some private protection work," Longarm said with a yawn because he was not the least bit ruffled by Billy's outburst. "The money is too good to turn down."

"Who do you think you are going to protect against whom?" Billy asked, leaning back in his office chair and kicking his feet up on his big walnut desk. "Because I don't think I can allow you to do this."

Longarm had been sitting down in his boss's office, but now he came to his feet, removed a cigar from his coat pocket and stuck it in the corner of his mouth unlit. He reflectively chewed on the cigar for a moment, his long brown handlebar mustache twitching with annoyance. "Look Billy, how many years have I worked for you?"

"I don't know. At least ten."

"Close enough. And have I ever asked for time off so that I can supplement the paltry salary I'm being paid?"

"No, but . . ."

"And haven't I always taken every crummy assignment you've handed out with a cheerful smile?"

"Sometimes you weren't all that cheerful."

"Sure, but only because you sent me to places like Yuma, Arizona, in July or Casper in January when it was so cold a man's nose froze like an icicle."

"Okay." Billy threw up his hands. "I admit that you are my most reliable and best officer. You get assigned all the hard cases because I know you can handle them when no one else in this office can."

"Then let me do this job," Longarm said, not wanting to butt heads with a man he liked and respected. "I'll be protecting Miss Lilly Claire, the famous singer, from an assassin. He vows to kill her . . . if she doesn't submit to his demands for sexual favors."

Billy was puritanical and easily offended when it came to the honor of women. "The cad! The monster!"

"My sentiments exactly. I've seen the notes that are being sent to Miss Claire. They're enough to make a grown man's blood run cold, let alone that of a lady."

Billy shook his head. "What is this world coming to? Used to be women were respected and rightly so. Custis, do you think the man who is threatening Miss Claire is serious about his threats, or is he just another crackpot?"

"I think he is *very* serious," Longarm replied. "But how can anyone be sure? Lilly is beautiful, famous and desirable and . . ."

"*Lilly?* You're calling Miss Claire by her *first* name?"

"Sure, why not?"

Billy well knew the appeal that Longarm posed for women. His peccadilloes were as legendary as his gunfights. "And does Lilly call you Custis? Or does she call you . . . well, never mind what she probably calls you."

Billy sighed. "Don't tell me. You've already seduced the woman."

"I didn't *seduce* Lilly!" Longarm protested with righteous indignation. "If anything, Lilly seduced *me*. Not only with her obvious endowments, but with this generous temporary job offer."

"How much is she offering to pay you?" Billy asked, dropping his feet to the floor and leaning forward with great interest.

"Five hundred for a week to protect her before she leaves town. Five hundred more, if I catch or kill the son of a bitch threatening her life."

Billy whistled softly. "That is a lot of money."

"Of course it is," Longarm said, taking his seat again. "It's too tempting for me to pass up. And besides, if I did pass it up and she hired some incompetent joker who allowed her to be shot . . . then I'd never forgive myself. And neither would you, boss."

Billy relaxed and almost grinned. "Custis," he said, "don't try to lay guilt on me. What I'm saying is that you are a federal officer of the law. Not some private bodyguard for hire. I'm just not sure that I can legally allow you to take this job."

Longarm's brow furrowed. "And I'm not sure you can legally prevent me from taking some long overdue vacation time and using that time as I wish. In fact . . . in fact, I'll insist on using my vacation time as I wish."

Billy's expression turned grim. "Just so we're clear on this, are you giving me an ultimatum?"

Longarm didn't want to put it that way, even if that was exactly what he was doing. "Billy, I'm saying that I really need this extra money. I've got into some debts that the five hundred would more than eliminate. After I pay those off, I might even open a bank savings account. You know, and make interest on my savings?"

"Ha!" Billy laughed. "The day you save a dime is the day that hell freezes over."

"Billy, Billy," Longarm said, trying to look offended. "I'm getting older and wiser. I'm starting to look to the future. I can't be running after criminals for the rest of my life. Dodging bullets and sharp knives. I might even decide that it's time to take a desk job, a position of respect and authority like you."

"Spare me the bullshit!" Billy cried. "You've told me a hundred times that you'd rather be dipped in hot tar than sit in an office."

"I know," Longarm said, "but a man can change. My landlord has been giving me a hard time lately. I'm thinking, if I can arrest whoever it is that is threatening Lilly and earn that thousand dollars, I might invest in a little house."

"What?" Billy's face showed his disbelief.

"I'm serious," Longarm said. "This town is booming. More people coming in every day. Housing prices can't help but go up and I think I need to get into the market while I still can."

Billy leaned back and laced his fingers behind his head. He was of average size but graying with a comfortable pot belly and jowls. "Custis, you are really layin' it on thick today. Savings account. Housing market? If this weren't a serious discussion, I'd be doubled up with laughter."

"Well," Longarm said, "if you think it's funny, that's your privilege, I guess. But I am in debt and I will save some of the money for a rainy day. So how about it, Billy?"

"Did you suggest to Miss Claire that this is a job for the Denver police department?"

"I did, but she doesn't apparently have much faith in them."

"All right," Billy said, "you've got the week off. Fill out the paperwork, but just between us, I wouldn't mention that you are putting your gun and skills out for hire. It could cause us some problems that we don't need."

"Good advice," Longarm said, unable to hide his sense of relief. He started for the door. "Thanks, boss."

"You're welcome. But Custis?"

"Yeah?"

"If this blows up in your face and my superiors realize what you've been doing this next week, we could all have our butts in the wringer. And by that, I mean, if you or Miss Claire are killed or injured by this nut case."

"I understand."

"The wise thing to do would be to bring in the police department . . . or for Miss Claire to just cancel her performances and leave Denver."

"I suggested the latter idea and she told me that the man writing the notes promised he'd follow her wherever she travels. So you see that we might as well do our best to catch and put him away. Or put him under."

"Arrest him, if you can. Kill him only if you must."

"Sure, boss."

Billy shook his head. "You're going to kill him if you can. I know that and you know that. But think about the consequences and how it could affect both of our careers, if this blows up in a shit storm."

"I will," Longarm promised.

"Are you going to keep me posted?"

Longarm's hand was on the door. "I hadn't planned on it. After all, I will be using my vacation time."

Billy thought about that for a moment. "Yeah," he said, "that's probably best. But, if I don't see you coming through this door in a week, I'm going to know I should have insisted that you turn this job offer down."

"Oh," Longarm said feeling quite cheerful since he'd gotten his way, "you'll definitely see me in a week. And when you do, I'll be a man free of his debts and wearing a new suit, hat and boots. Yep, Billy, you'll see a prosperous man working for you where you used to see a poor one burdened by his debts."

"The shit is getting deep in here, Custis. Close the door behind you before I start to gag."

Longarm laughed and headed out to tell Lilly that, for the next week . . . or less if he killed her tormentor . . . he was going to be her main man.

Chapter 5

Longarm filled out the paperwork requesting a week of vacation time. He hated forms of any kind, especially government forms and wondered if the agency had gotten so big that a man couldn't just tell his boss and coworkers that he was leaving for a while. But no, there were forms to fill out and they would go to several departments. In the little section where the form asked where you would be spending your vacation, Longarm simply put "around town." That would be the truth even if it did seem a bit ridiculous to have a vacation without traveling anywhere new.

He gave the forms to Billy Vail's secretary and was about to leave when Billy called him back inside his office. His boss gave him a tight smile and said, "Just wanted to remind you to keep in touch. And, if there is an attempt on Miss Lilly Claire's life, then you had better cover your ass by immediately notifying the Denver police. They won't appreciate you keeping this matter secret and there is no need for hard feelings between our departments."

"You got it," Longarm said.

"What's she like?" Billy blurted.

He turned. "Miss Lilly?"

"I'm not talking about the wife of the President of the United States."

He shrugged. "She's okay."

"Just okay?" Billy asked.

"All right, she's better'n okay. Face of an angel and the voice to match. But she's not nearly as cuddly or soft as you might expect. In fact, I'd say that Lilly is pretty tough inside. She's probably had a lot of men try to take advantage of her fame and beauty. Lilly is tough and wary."

"Yeah, because having some nut case sending her notes about what he wants to do to her body is enough to make any woman a man-hater. And she must be pretty rich if she can offer you that much money."

"I suppose."

"So are you staying with her . . . or at your own apartment?"

"I don't know," Longarm replied. "We haven't gone over the details. I wanted to make sure I was cleared at this end before I accepted the job."

"Don't take her bullet," Billy warned. "And be smart. Get her out of town if you start to think her life is really in jeopardy."

"I need to finish this job for her. Give her some peace of mind. Everyone should have peace of mind, Billy. Even the rich and the famous."

"She sings beautifully, huh?"

"Yes, but I've heard better."

He raised his eyebrows in question. "Who?"

"My mother," Longarm said. "When I was growing up in West Virginia, she used to sing the old country songs born in the Appalachians. From my earliest memories, I can still hear her voice as sweet and clear as a church bell tolling on a snowy winter morning. And my father could play a mean fiddle."

"Why, that's a beautiful description, Custis! You never told me that you have a gifted musical background."

"You never asked." Longarm smiled with regret. "And besides, none of it rubbed off on me. I sound like a choking frog trying to sing and I couldn't carry a tune in a milk bucket."

Longarm went back to his apartment to check his mail and pack a small suitcase with enough fresh underwear and other personal items to last him at least a few days. In the mail he found several bills, all of them overdue. Instead of trashing them as he often did, Longarm placed the bills on his kitchen table believing that he would be able to pay them off in a week. It was a good feeling to think that he might finally be free of debt. And, if he made the thousand dollars, he really would open a savings account. Why, he'd even show Billy the proof of it just to make the man eat his sarcastic words.

Finished with his preparations, Longarm then headed for the Birdcage Theater to meet with Lilly. He found her in her dressing room, and she was in anything but an amorous mood. In fact, Lilly looked downright grave.

"I got another note," she said, extending it toward him. "This one is the most ominous yet. I'm really getting scared, Custis."

"Let me see it."

Longarm unfolded the note and read:

Dear Darling Lilly,

   I have grown tired of waiting for you to answer my fervent and passionate requests. Perhaps you think you are above me, a common man without

*fame or fortune. If so, I assure you that you are
making a fatal mistake.*

*If you do not agree to my request for a lover's
tryst, I will kill you in the next few days, possibly even
hours. Leave a note telling me of your decision today
at five o'clock. Leave it in the public park downtown
where the copper statue stands. Put the note between
the statue's feet and I will then tell you where we can
meet to explore each other's most intimate secrets.*

If there is no note . . . you will have no tomorrow.

Lilly was pacing back and forth in her dressing room.
"Every previous note he sent was at least civil. Pleading,
actually, but always with an underlying threat to my life.
But this time, he's come right out and promised to kill me
immediately, if I don't agree to meet with him."

Longarm studied the handwriting. It was a scrawling
and very untidy script. The tails of the ending letters of
each sentence were dramatic, unbalanced swirls without
grace or elegance. The letters themselves were not uniform in size and the capital letters were greatly exagger-
ated, like the ego of the man who had written this last,
threatening note. Longarm had always been interested in
handwriting and believed that a messy, scrawled handwriting was indicative of a messy, undisciplined mind.

This letter further enforced that theory.

"What are we to do?" Lilly asked, clearly rattled.

"We'll write a reply and place it at the feet of the
statue. Then, I'll hide and wait. When our crazy comes to
collect your note, I'll pounce on him and arrest the fiend.
It shouldn't be that difficult."

Lilly nodded and found pen and ink. She had some perfumed stationery and sat down at her dressing room table.

She was wearing a lavender dress with a floral pattern. Her hair was mussed and she looked strained and several years older than she had the day before. Longarm felt sorry for her and wished for nothing more than to put an end to this terrible fear that was upon her.

Lilly tried to inject some hopefulness in her voice which made the situation seem all the more desperate. "All right, Custis. I think your plan is our only hope. Now, what shall I write?"

"Tell him that you are actually lonely and in need of love."

Her head snapped up and she wailed, "What?"

"Just do it," Longarm ordered. "Tell him that you even admire his . . . his persistence and that anyone who loves you as much as he does can win your heart. And Lilly?"

"Yes?"

"Snip off a small lock of your hair."

"You must be kidding!" Her hand flew to her hair.

"Do it," Longarm said. "A man this obsessed will, of course, believe anything you write. He will read your note a thousand times. And perhaps even pleasure himself with his own hand, so great will be his passion."

"Oh, please, Custis. Must I really . . ."

"A lock of your hair. Then write, Lilly. Put it in your own words, but tell him essentially what I've just said. Trust me."

Lilly sat down and wrote the message. Longarm could see that she struggled yet finished the onerous task. "How should I end this letter?"

"Tell him to come to your dressing room after tonight's performance. Tell him to come very late. Midnight would be perfect when everyone but yourself is gone."

"But why should I do that if you're going to catch him at the fountain?"

39

"Back up in case he doesn't show at the park today," Longarm said. "This just gives us added insurance."

She nodded her head stiffly. "Good idea."

Lilly finished the note and then found scissors. She snipped off a small lock of her hair, clearly upset at giving her tormentor even this small part of herself. Then she placed the lock and note into an envelope and handed it to Longarm who told her, "No, Lilly. This man is crazy, but he's probably very cunning. There's not a doubt in my mind that he'll be watching the statue all day. He's probably there right now, hidden among the usual daytime crowd. However, if someone other than yourself delivers the note, he'll become suspicious and much harder to trap. You have to deliver it yourself."

"But I'll be recognized by the people in the plaza! I'll be mobbed and then how can I possibly slip this note onto the statue?"

"You'll have to be disguised enough so that the public will not recognize you, but that this crazy man will. Can you do that?"

"I suppose, but . . ."

"There's no time to waste," Longarm interrupted. "Let's get you ready and I'll be close by when you arrive at the park. After you leave the note, get back in your carriage and return here without deviation. Be sure and lock the door. Post a guard."

"Edward will be with me whenever you're not," she told him.

"Fine." Longarm looked at her closely. "Have you told him yet about our financial arrangement?"

"No. But I did get the cash." She reached into a drawer and under some papers. She brought the money out and studied it for a moment. "Custis, do you want part of it now? Say, half in good faith?"

Longarm considered this offer with care. If he failed and Lilly were killed—a thought he could scarcely allow himself to imagine—then he'd get nothing. On the other hand, his honor told him he would certainly not deserve a penny if he failed in his duty.

"No," he said. "Hold on to the cash."

Her smile was immediate and genuine. "I was hoping that would be your answer. It tells me that you have a great deal of confidence in yourself to protect me from harm."

"I *am* confident." Longarm went over and kissed Lilly on the lips. Then, he prepared to leave. "I'll be at the park. It would be best if we are not seen together this week."

"I understand."

"Good. I'll be at the park watching."

She chewed nervously on her lower lip. "You don't think he'd be crazy enough to try and . . ."

"No," Longarm interrupted. "He wants you alive. He wants you naked in his arms moaning and telling him what a man he is instead of what a miserable little snake. He wants to . . . well, you can guess."

"Please, Custis, I don't want to think about it."

"I understand."

Longarm left her then and headed for the park with the statue. The park wasn't large or even impressive, but it was always crowded on warm summer days because it had a pond with ducks and the water gave the impression of cool serenity. Children played on swings while young lovers strolled, lost in their romantic reverie. Old men played cribbage and poker for peanuts and pennies. Lonely singles sat on park benches waiting for the answer to their prayers, which probably never appeared.

In addition to that, dogs of all sizes and descriptions ran, played, fornicated and fought. The statue was situated directly in the center of the park. About eight feet tall and

41

made of bronze turning green, it was a tribute to someone once important but already forgotten. Longarm remembered the statue had been defaced and where the mouth was, there often jutted the stub of a cheap cigar which was sad but also amusing. No one really remembered who the rich man was because his name was obscured by a deep layer of pigeon shit.

Chapter 6

Longarm took a roundabout way to the park and then he joined the afternoon crowd. He bought a bag of peanuts from a vendor to feed the squirrels and was careful to attract no undue attention. That wasn't easy, however, because of his height and good looks. Young women gave him first and then second glances but he paid them no attention. Rather, he kept his head turned slightly downward as he studied the dozens of faces trying to guess who Lilly's tormentor might be.

When Lilly appeared, he didn't even recognize her until she was almost to the statue. She had assumed the look of a working woman and had made herself appear downright unattractive. Part of it was that she had affected a slight stoop as if she were a poor working girl who had long carried heavy burdens. She wore a shapeless dress and probably some padding to make her look big in the hips and decidedly dowdy. And on her feet she wore a pair of ragged slippers. She had even smeared dirt or dust on her face and arms.

But no one could mistake Lilly's long, lustrous black

hair. That was the giveaway, the thing that would identify her to the man who had sent the threatening notes. He alone among all these people would know that the real Lilly Claire was in the park delivering a reply to his note.

"Good job!" Longarm said to himself as he slipped in behind a large tree where he would be hidden from view yet close enough to collar Lilly's stalker the moment he first appeared.

Lilly shuffled to the statue and sat down at its base on a little stone bench. She kept her head down to avoid anyone recognizing her although Longarm felt that was unnecessary because she was so well disguised.

Now, Longarm watched as she surreptitiously removed a note from her dress and placed it between the feet of the anonymous Denver patriarch. Lilly was waiting for something to happen and so was Longarm. But the next few minutes passed without incident. Then the next hour. Longarm could see that Lilly was growing impatient and yet he could do nothing but hide in wait and watch the people in the park.

There were some old men at a park table playing cards. Women, children and some men. A few dogs but not a single person who looked to be a potential killer.

Longarm grew weary of the wait. He tried to signal to Lilly that she should leave the park, but he couldn't catch her eye. Taking a deep breath, Longarm checked his pocket watch and determined that nearly two hours had passed since Lilly's appearance. Maybe the man they wanted had decided to wait until dark.

Longarm moved out of his cover. He strolled casually toward the statue, a lazy smile on his lips as if his thoughts were a million miles away. When he got near Lilly, he bent as though to retrieve something he had dropped. Still not looking at Lilly, he whispered, "Go ahead and leave. I'll remain here for a few more hours. Great disguise!"

Head still down, she said nothing but did as she was told. Longarm straightened up as Lilly moved off. But just then, out of the corner of his eye, he saw a blur and felt an alarm bell sound in his brain.

"Lilly!" he shouted when she was forty feet away and leaving the park.

At that instant and just as he was spinning around to face the danger, he heard the gunshots, felt the pain and then the numbness. As he dropped he saw the terrible image of a man dressed in a black suit taking aim at Lilly and shooting her. He tried to cry out in warning but it was all too late. He was down, and just before he struck the grass, he saw Lilly's chest erupt in crimson as the assassin's bullets found her heart.

Longarm was awakened in surgery. He seemed to be in a deep well of pain and misery from which there was no escape.

"Hold on to life, Marshal!" the surgeon implored. "We're going to get this bullet out and you're going to make it. Just don't give up on us now!"

Longarm tried to tell the doctor that he had no intention of "giving up" and that he had been shot many times and had always survived. But the doctor probably knew that already because Longarm was essentially naked with only a green sheet over his lower body that left exposed all the scars on his torso.

"All right," the surgeon said, his voice tight with anxiety as he turned to an assistant. "Hold him still. I've almost got the second bullet. Just a little more and . . . there!"

But Longarm had lost consciousness slipping back into that well of darkness.

He awoke with Billy Vail hovering overheard. "Custis? Custis, can you hear me?"

Longarm's eyes popped open and he saw Billy as if through murky water. He blinked several times and finally nodded as Billy's image clarified. "Hey, boss. What . . ."

"The doctor said that you need to conserve your strength. But we need to know what happened from your perspective. We have interviewed many witnesses to the double shooting. But no one seems to agree on the description of who gunned down you and Miss Claire."

"Is she dead?"

"Near death. She's in even more critical condition than you are. The doctors are giving her less than a fifty-fifty chance."

Longarm was crushed by the realization that he had failed. Failed miserably and completely to protect that beautiful woman.

"I need to see her."

"No point in that," Billy said. "She's unconscious. She took three rounds and has lost so much blood that the doctors say it would be a near miracle if she survives. I'm afraid that Miss Claire is hardly recognizable."

"She was disguised as a poor working woman."

"That explains it then. Custis, did you see the face of the man with the gun?"

"No," Longarm whispered, replaying it all in his mind again. How had he been so negligent? How could something as horrible as this have happened?

Billy leaned closer. "Witnesses say he was young and about six feet tall. Good-looking but wild-eyed. When he opened fire, first on you and then Miss Claire, he then turned and fired a shot at those nearest to him. Everyone panicked, of course, and some even dove into the pond seeking safety. Others simply ran. The fact of the matter is, no one can quite agree on anything more than what I've just told you. He was young, dressed in a black suit, about six feet tall and handsome. That description could fit *hundreds* of men in this town."

Longarm closed his eyes and tried to concentrate on the split second when he'd seen the assassin. But it was all a blur. No more than a smeared image overridden by the sound of repeated gunfire and his own helplessness and pain.

"Maybe I'll remember more later," he said, doubting it. "But I need to see Lilly."

"You can't do that," Billy said, placing his hand on Longarm's shoulder. "You're in very bad shape. Lilly's fate is out of our hands. You must rest and recover. I'm going to put every man I can spare on this case and I'm sure that the Denver police department will do the same. Especially if Miss Claire doesn't recover."

Longarm grated his teeth in rage and frustration. "Billy, I failed her."

"You should never have taken this case. I blame myself as much as you for what happened. I should have insisted that you turn down the offer."

"I wouldn't have listened to you," Longarm whispered. "I thought that I could protect her. I thought that I was the only one good enough to protect Lilly!"

"Everyone fails now and then," Billy said, his expression bleak. "Maybe it's time you thought about a desk job. I just hope to be able to keep the fact that you were freelancing from the media. They'll have a great time with that and you'll go from being a hero who just happened to get in the way of a crazy man's bullets, to a fool who failed his duty. If the truth comes out, we'll all take heat from this one."

"This was *my* decision," Longarm said. "And I won't let your career be damaged because of my failure."

"Let's not talk about this anymore," Billy said. "What is done is done and the only thing we can do is to pray for Miss Claire to have a complete recovery and to try and catch the bloody bastard who shot you both."

Longarm managed to nod his head in agreement. But already, he was determined that he would rise from this hospital bed and take up the hunt for the man dressed in black.

It was the least he could do having utterly failed his mission.

Chapter 7

Three days had passed during which time Longarm was in and out of consciousness. When he finally felt as if he could think clearly and even rise from his hospital bed, Longarm decided that he *had* to see Lilly Claire. No one was telling him anything about her condition and it was driving him crazy.

"What are you doing, Mr. Long?" a nurse cried when she happened to glance into his room and see him with his feet on the floor. "Get back in that bed."

"Not until I've seen someone."

"You're not going to see anyone."

Longarm tried to stand up straight, but his head began to spin and he got dizzy. The next thing he knew he was back on the bed and then he remembered nothing.

He awoke in the middle of the night feeling stronger and even more determined that he would get out of the bed and visit Lilly. Maybe she'd had a few more seconds to see their attacker and he needed all the help he could get, if he was going to stop this killer. Longarm determined that, this time, he would sneak out of his private hospital room and down the hall. He knew that the women's ward was on the second floor. If he could manage to climb the stairs, he could slip up to Lilly's room and have a few words with her and apologize for his failure. He recalled someone saying that she was in Room 204 and that shouldn't be too difficult to find. With luck, the nurses would be in their station and they'd never see him.

Longarm took several deep breaths, then he climbed out of bed and found his clothes. Since he was stiff and sore, he didn't bother with his socks and shoes. Getting his pants and shirt on was hard enough and he felt a little shaky by the time he was ready to leave.

The staircase wasn't very far from his room and he made it there easily enough. But climbing the stairs to the second floor was kind of tough. He had to keep stopping to rest and he was sweating and feeling a bit woozy by the time he got to the top.

The women's ward was a dimly lit hallway with a polished linoleum floor shining under a row of soft lights. At the far end of the hall, he could hear women in conversation and the light was much brighter. Longarm was sure this was where the nurses gathered and kept the patient records.

He tiptoed down the hallway with his right hand brushing the wall to steady himself. Each room was numbered and he was sure glad when he reached Room 204.

Entering the room, he saw that its window shades were open and there was barely enough light to see Lilly's outline resting on the bed. She was snoring quite loudly with her mouth wide open.

My gawd, she sure does look old and weak, Longarm thought as he moved across the room and then stopped beside the bed.

"Lilly?"

She kept snoring so he reached over to touch her on the shoulder. "Lilly, it's me. Marshal Long. Wake up!"

Lilly snorted with surprise and her eyes flew open. She blinked and screamed. It was a high-pitched, terrified scream that sent Longarm reeling back toward the door. But he tripped over something and fell hard.

He was awakened moments later by the shouts of nurses and Lilly's shrill screaming.

"What are you doing up here?" a big nurse demanded with her hands on her heavy hips.

When he didn't immediately answer, Longarm was pulled roughly to his bare feet. "Let go of me. I'm a patient down below. Room 106. Marshal Long. I need to talk to Miss Claire. I said to let go of me, dammit!"

"Miss Claire isn't here anymore."

This caught Longarm off guard. "Then where in blazes is she?"

Two nurses escorted Longarm out of the room while a third stayed with the screaming woman. Longarm was confused and upset. "Dammit," he shouted in exasperation, "where'd you put her?"

"She's in the *morgue*, Marshal Long. Miss Lilly Claire passed over the bar two days ago."

"What?" Longarm couldn't believe it.

"That's right," the nurse said, almost acting triumphant to see him so shaken. "And *you're* a candidate to do the same, if you don't stick to your bed!"

Longarm shrugged off her arm and leaned heavily against the wall. "Are you certain that Lilly died?"

"Of course. We really never thought Miss Claire had a chance."

Longarm wheeled around and headed for the staircase, but the nurses caught him and forced him into an empty room. "Marshal, you're going to have to stay here until we can get a doctor to examine you. You might have torn open your wounds and you could bleed to death because of your own stupidity."

"You're a real Florence Nightingale, aren't you?" he said sarcastically.

She placed her big hands on her wide hips and glared at him. "Don't give me any of your lip, buster!"

Longarm was pushed into an empty room and made to remove his clothes and then lie down on a bed. No one was in a mood to tuck him in for the rest of the night and he would have punched one of them if they had tried.

"Do we need to restrain you, Marshal?" the big nurse in charge asked, coming into his room.

"You mean sit on me?"

"No," she shot back, "I was thinking of strapping you to the bed. We do that in cases of severe dementia ... which I'm beginning to think you might have."

Longarm was covered with a cold sweat from his exertions, but he was still a man and he damn sure didn't appreciate being talked to like a truant child. "Nurse," he warned, "you try to strap me down, and I'll get those straps and whip your fat ass until you won't be able to sit for a week!"

The big nurse actually growled a moment before she whirled and fled his room.

"And shut the door behind you!" Longarm bellowed.

"Go to hell, Marshal!"

"I've already been there and back."

The door to his little room slammed shut and Longarm was plunged into darkness. But this time, his mind was clear and he knew another kind of hell.

Miss Lilly Claire was *dead*!

Longarm lay awake for the rest of the night trying to think of how he would track down the assassin that had killed Lilly and had almost killed him. He would begin by interviewing Edward . . . hell, maybe he was the one that had been sending Lilly those crazy notes. Edward fit the description of the shooter, and Longarm was almost certain that he was a lot more to Lilly than a half brother. Most likely, he was a sometimes lover and full-time personal assistant to the famous singer.

That would explain his aloofness that bordered on outright hostility when he had met a rival for Lilly's attention. And Longarm had been that rival.

Yes, Longarm decided, the more he thought about it, *Edward whatever his last name is will be my prime suspect.*

That decided, Longarm drifted off to sleep just as the sun was coming up in the east. He was still sleeping at ten o'clock that morning in the women's ward when Billy Vail appeared with one of his other senior marshals, a taciturn man named Dan Hooker. Hooker resented Longarm because he was given the most difficult office cases. Longarm thought Hooker was a jerk ever since the day he'd caught the marshal beating the hell out of an old drunk while trying to extract some information on a robbery case.

"Custis, we heard you created quite a stir upstairs last night," Billy said.

Longarm wasn't interested in the subject. "Why didn't you tell me about Lilly dying two days ago?"

"I didn't think you needed the extra grief," Billy said.

"I expect you to be forthright and honest. What the hell kind of nonsense are you pulling on me?"

"Easy," Billy said, raising his hands up. "Get too excited and you could split your stitches."

"The hell with that," Longarm told him. "I deserved to know about Lilly's death and you didn't tell me."

"I'm sorry. Okay?"

It wasn't okay but Longarm decided to let it pass. He turned his attention to the other marshal. "What are you doing here, Dan? I don't see any roses or candy in your hands and you probably aren't too worried about my health."

"I'm taking over one of your old cases," Hooker told him with a sneer. "Thought I might get some information that you *failed* to include in your case documentation."

"What case?" Longarm asked.

"The Alfred Winslow case."

Longarm just stared at Hooker, but then he almost laughed. "Is *that* the case that you've been assigned?"

"Sure," Hooker said defensively. "You never solved that one so I figured to do it for you."

"Very good!" Longarm exclaimed, turning to Billy. "That's an extremely interesting case."

"Sure it is," Hooker said, looking smug. "I'm going over all the old information. I'm going to start contacting witnesses again."

"Is that a fact?" Longarm said.

"Yep. And I'll bet I solve the case within a month."

"Well," Longarm said, humoring him. "That sure does sound promising."

"Custis, behave yourself," Billy warned.

"Oh, I will," Longarm promised, trying to look sincere. "But Billy, is it possible that you don't remember Alfred Winslow admitted that he faked his own murder? We know that because Winslow was caught and arrested last year in a San Francisco brothel with nearly six thousand dollars of bank money still in his possession."

Billy gulped, then slapped his forehead and rolled his eyes. "Come to think of it, I do remember now that you mention it." He turned to Hooker. "Dan, I'm sure sorry about that. I'll think of another case you can handle."

Hooker blushed with humiliation and that made Longarm feel a whole lot better. So he asked, "When is Lilly's funeral?"

"Tomorrow. Ought to be a big affair. Lots of fans and the newspapers. It'll be a circus."

"I'll be there," Longarm vowed. "The way I see it, it's the least I can do for the woman."

"Now, Custis, I doubt the doctor will allow that."

"Doesn't matter," Longarm said, "because I'm checking out of this place first thing tomorrow morning."

"You never learn."

"I learn," he answered. "Years ago I learned that hospitals are death houses where people very often die of infections they've caught from other patients."

"I don't think that's one bit true," Hooker argued.

"What you think means nothing," Longarm replied. "Get out of this room. You're a walking infection."

Hooker was big man, but slow and clumsy. He looked stupid and actually was. Now, however, he just wanted to get in the last word. "There'll come a day when we settle things once and for all between us."

Longarm said, "We could do it right now."

"You're in no shape to fight."

"That's why you might have a Chinaman's chance," Longarm told the man. "Now disappear."

Hooker stomped into the hallway.

Billy looked peeved. "You shouldn't bait him that way."

"And you shouldn't try to give him my old cases. How is young Jed Connor doing on the job?"

"He resigned yesterday. I was shocked. Jed came into my office first thing in the morning and handed in his badge."

"Did he offer you a reason why?"

"He just decided that being a lawman just wasn't his cup of tea."

Longarm wasn't a bit surprised. "Actually, I'm glad to hear that he resigned. The kid would have gotten killed sooner or later. He didn't have the personality or instincts to make a good United States Marshal. What young Jed Connor needs is to find a nice, safe job and get married. Raise a family and grow old."

"Maybe so," Billy agreed. "But now I'm real short-handed. How soon are you coming back? A month or two?"

"Give me a week or two," Longarm told him. "I heal fast because I've had so much practice at it."

Billy went over to the window. "Are you really going to try and attend Lilly Claire's funeral?"

"I wouldn't miss it for the world."

"You shouldn't go."

"I must."

"Then I'll come by and pick you up in a carriage."

"Thanks, Billy. And tell Dan Hooker not to show."

"He's really not all that bad. Dan gets along fine with my other marshals. I don't know why you and he have such an intense dislike for each other."

"He's a rotten apple, Billy. And some day, he'll pull some crazy shenanigan and kill an innocent man. In case you haven't noticed, Dan Hooker enjoys inflicting serious pain. He's a sadist."

"And you're a loose cannon. Do you have any idea how hard it was for me to get the fact that you were working for Lilly covered up with the brass?"

"No."

"Well, it wasn't easy. And, if the press catches wind of it, I'll probably be sent off on permanent duty to patrol our border with Mexico riding a gawdamn burro."

Longarm had to chuckle. "If that happens, I'll go along with you."

"Small comfort," Billy groused. "Miss Claire's funeral is at ten o'clock and there'll be a huge crowd. I'll pick you up at nine."

"I'll be ready. But Billy?"

The man turned at the door. "Yeah?"

"Did you *really* forget about the Winslow case being solved?"

Billy blushed with embarrassment. "My mind has been distracted with other matters lately. And you've been one of them. So let's forget it. Okay?"

"Sure," Longarm said. "Don't get sore. I was just curious."

"Yeah," Billy said. "And stay the hell away from Nurse Gorkley."

"Is she that ugly gorilla in charge upstairs?"

"That's the one."

"She needs to give herself a big *enema*. Better yet, tell Nurse Gorkley that I'll gladly do it for her with a borrowed fireman's hose."

Longarm could hear Billy's laughter echo clear down the hall.

Chapter 8

Longarm hated funerals, but this funeral was different from any he'd ever attended. In the first place, it was by far the largest and Longarm guessed that there were at least five hundred people. But no one was crying or even mourning, which was the strangest thing, until Longarm realized that nearly everyone here was nothing more than a curious spectator. And there were lots of newspaper people. The casket was white and it must have cost a small fortune when you added in all the floral arrangements and the fancy carriage with six black horses that waited to take the famous Miss Lilly Claire to the cemetery.

"This is even more impressive than the late Governor Tadbury's funeral," Billy whispered as they sat in a pew at the rear of the huge Methodist church. "And his coffin wouldn't hold a candle to this one."

Longarm nodded in agreement even though he had not attended the governor's funeral.

"And," Billy continued, "look at all the flowers. I should have brought my wife. She loves flowers and would have really been impressed."

"I expect so."

"Well, it's for certain that you and I will never go out with such grand style," Billy said. "Not that it matters after you're dead."

"No, it sure doesn't."

"Look! There's Senator Bolton and his wife."

"I noticed." Longarm wished that Billy would be quiet. People were beginning to turn around and glare at them.

"And over there. Isn't that Mr. Stanton, the largest property holder in all of Denver?"

"I wouldn't know," Longarm said. "What really interests me is who isn't here."

And that would be?"

"Lilly's half brother, Edward."

"Last name?"

"I don't know. She never told me."

"Well," Billy said, "maybe the poor man is simply too overcome with grief to attend."

"It's possible," Longarm conceded, "although Edward didn't strike me as the faint or wilting kind."

"Perhaps he'll show up late, then. Or at the cemetery."

"Or not at all," Longarm mused.

The minister in his flowing robes was suitably late and the church was baking hot by the time that he mounted the altar.

"Senator Bolton. Mrs. Bolton. Ladies and gentlemen. We are gathered here to commemorate the celebrity of one of America's brightest stars. A star dimmed all too soon, but one who shone so brilliantly in God's favor. Miss Lilly Claire was . . ."

Longarm didn't hear any more. He was tired from lack of sleep at the hospital, and besides, he'd heard the sermon dozens of times and wasn't all that interested. It wasn't that he was disdainful or irreligious; he just simply didn't think that God listened to man very closely. There were too many human beings whining and down on their knees praying for the most trivial and ridiculous things that if God listened to everything, he'd be overloaded. So, to Longarm's way of thinking, he probably only heard prayers for really big things like epidemics, wars and such. Not the death of every person and their favorite personal cause.

He must have dozed off because he was sweating like a horse when Billy finally nudged him and whispered, "Nice going, Custis. You started to snore and everyone in the church turned around to see who was so rude."

"Sorry. Is it over?"

"Yes. And I have to tell you that you missed a very fine sermon. Why, there is hardly a dry eye in the whole church."

Longarm yawned and looked around. He saw that Billy wasn't exaggerating. "It was a real tearjerker, huh?"

"It sure was. What a tragedy that someone so talented and beautiful would be shot down in the prime of her life and career."

"Yeah," Longarm said, wondering if anyone would think to remark that *he* was almost cut down in the prime of his career. Not that law officers were so special that most cared. "It's a crying shame. And it sure is suffocating in here, Billy. Must be about a hundred degrees and not a whiff of fresh air. I'm really sweating."

"Be glad that you still can sweat, Custis. Lilly can't anymore, you know."

Longarm didn't think that was a kind remark, but he let it pass.

He watched as the pastor and his assistants left the altar

and came marching solemnly down the aisle. When they passed, Longarm smelled incense and he was starting to feel like he might need to toss his breakfast.

"Billy, I've got to get some fresh air *now*."

"Oh, for heaven's sake!" Billy cried as Longarm lurched out of the pew and practically knocked over some of the pastor's assistants in his rush to get fresh air and his worry about tossing his last meal on someone.

The carriage rolled off to the cemetery and everyone stood on the stairs watching, not a word being spoken. Finally, one of the pastor's accomplices announced that everyone could go to the cemetery.

And a few actually did. But most had had enough of the somber business and with their morbid curiosities satisfied, they drifted away chattering and wiping their sweaty brows.

"I'll take you back to your apartment now," Billy said. "Your color is alarming."

"I would like to lie down and rest," Longarm admitted.

"I'll go get our carriage and be back as soon as I can," Billy promised. "Why don't you sit down on that bench in the shade? Really, Custis, you shouldn't have come. I told you that, but you just wouldn't listen. You *never* listen."

"Piss off, Billy. I'm in no mood for a damned lecture."

Longarm went over to the bench. It was already occupied by a heavyset couple whose faces were flushed from the heat. Ordinarily, Longarm would have found some other spot to rest, but not today.

"Would you both mind scooting down a little bit? I need to sit down."

The middle-aged couple gave him a look as if to say he was impossibly rude, but Longarm gave them a drop-dead stare and they got up and left muttering.

Longarm took a few deep breaths and bent his head

down. He sure didn't want to get sick in public, but a foul taste was boiling in his gut and he didn't know if he could keep his light breakfast down.

"I need a cigar," he said to himself. And, fortunately, he had one in his coat pocket. He didn't waste any time with the usual preliminaries. He just bit off the tip, stuck the cigar in his mouth and had it lit and puffing in seconds.

The cigar smoke did settle his stomach or maybe it gave his stomach something else to consider. Either way, he felt better after a few moments and mopped the cold sweat from his brow.

"Excuse me?"

Longarm glanced up to see a young man of perhaps fifteen years old. He was scruffy looking but wore a very earnest expression. "Sir," he said, "aren't you that lawman that Miss Lilly hired to protect her?"

"Who are you?"

"I'm nobody," the kid replied. "But I knew Miss Claire and I would run errands for her while she was backstage. She was very generous to me, a poor urchin of the streets."

"What is your name?"

"I'd rather not say, sir."

The boy looked scared and there were fresh tears on his cheeks. Longarm softened his voice. "It appears to me that you are one of the few here that really are mourning Miss Claire's death."

"That's not quite right, sir."

"Then what is right?" Longarm asked. "Speak up, boy. I'm not feeling any too chipper and there will be a carriage around in a few moments to pick me up. Did Miss Lilly owe you money and now you're in a tight fix? Is that it?"

"No sir! I . . . oh, never mind."

The boy turned to leave but something about his face and tone of voice made Longarm reach out and grab him by the arm. "Boy," he said, "you came here to tell me something. If it's a few dollars you need, then ask and I'll give them to you."

"It's not the money, sir! It's far more than that."

"Then what is it? Speak up."

"You wouldn't send me to jail, sir. Would you now?"

"What's your *name*?"

"Wilbur," he stammered. "Wilbur Riley."

"What did you do, Wilbur, steal some of the lady's precious things?"

"No!" Wilbur looked aghast. "I swear by all that is holy that I didn't steal from Miss Claire. Sir, I'm an orphan and poor as a church mouse, of that you can be sure. But I don't steal from them that treat me fairly and with kindness."

Longarm didn't need to be told that Wilbur was a boy of the streets without funds and probably without much of a future. And he could see by the kid's sunken cheeks and worn-out clothes that Wilbur was desperately poor. "Then what is this all about?"

"You might think I'm either crazy or a liar, if I tell you."

"If you don't tell me, I'm going to get mad."

"All right." Wilbur was wearing a cap and now he removed it and asked, "Can I sit down beside you in the shade, sir. I'm very hot."

"Sit."

"Sir, what I want to tell you might seem unbelievable. But I swear it to be the truth."

"Why don't you just spit it out and let me decide," Longarm told the kid as he tried to curb his impatience.

"Well, sir. It's . . . it's this. I could be wrong, but I think I saw Miss Claire leaving in a carriage early this morning."

"That's impossible!"

"Yes, sir. Impossible. That's what I thought. But I was going through the trash cans out behind the Birdcage Theater early this morning, like always, when I saw Mr. Hardy and . . ."

"Who is Mr. Hardy?" Longarm interrupted.

"Mr. Edward Hardy. Miss Claire's half brother. Only I don't think he is actually related to Miss Claire. Anyway, I saw them early this morning leave the dressing room and slip away in a coach."

Longarm just stared at Wilbur. "Miss Claire has been dead for several days. She was shot down by the same hand that shot me. It was in the newspapers."

"I can't read, sir. But I heard about the shooting and how you were both taken to the hospital. I prayed for you both. And when I heard Miss Claire had shipped out, why I cried like a baby."

The youth fell silent.

Longarm waited and then said, "Wilbur. Sometimes, when people are suffering from real loss, their grief is such that they can't think straight. They see or imagine they see things that don't exist. You shouldn't feel ashamed. You just saw something that wasn't there."

Wilbur nodded. "Maybe so. I don't know. They didn't see me. I hid, me being ashamed of going through the trash cans. I didn't want them to see that. But while I may not have much, I do have good eyes, sir. In fact, I have very good eyes. I can see tiny birds in the sky and other things that most people miss. I can spot a coin lying in the gutter on the next block. Yes, sir, I can do that. And I know that my eyes did not deceive me this morning."

The boy spoke with such conviction that Longarm took him seriously. "Perhaps, Wilbur, you saw someone that looked like Miss Claire."

"And another that looked like Mr. Hardy? Two mistakes? No, sir. I know what I saw and what I saw was the two of them getting into a coach and hurrying away."

"Miss Claire is in a fine casket. A casket that is being placed in the earth even as we speak."

"The casket may be going into the earth, sir. And it may well contain a body. But that body is not Miss Claire, thank God! Of that I am very, very certain."

Longarm was stumped. He just didn't know what to think. And just then, Billy's carriage arrived and his boss was waving him to hurry.

"Billy," Longarm said, "do you know the location of the cemetery where Miss Claire is to be buried?"

"Yes, sir. It's the Eternal Rest Cemetery out past Cherry Creek."

"That's right," Longarm said, then he turned to the boy. "Go there and mark where the burial takes place. Then stay there until later this evening."

"May I ask what for, sir?"

"Oh, and find a shovel."

"Why don't you just go stop the buryin' now, sir? Wouldn't that be easier?"

"Yes," Longarm said, "it would be. But, if you're wrong and Miss Claire is buried there, then we can simply recover the casket and no one will be much the wiser. We'll have satisfied our curiosities and not made fools out of ourselves."

"And if I'm right and Miss Claire isn't in that casket?"

"Then, Wilbur, I'll pay you a very handsome sum."

"I could use the money," Wilbur said, "but that's not what brought me to you."

"I know that," Longarm told the young man. "And I'll see you tonight at the grave."

"Should I start digging as soon as the sun goes down?"

"Only if no one is around," Longarm instructed. "But,

under no circumstances, do you open the casket. Is that clear?"

Wilbur actually shivered. "Don't you worry yourself any about that, sir. I wouldn't open that casket in the dark to save my soul!"

"Good," Longarm said. "Tonight then."

"Tonight with a shovel," Wilbur said. "I'll be there although it spooks me something terrible to be alone in a graveyard at night."

"You won't be there alone for long. That's my promise."

They shook hands on that and Longarm hurried over to the waiting carriage.

"Everything all right?" Billy asked.

"Fine."

"Who was that poor kid and why did you shake his hand?"

"He needed a little help, that's all," Longarm said, deciding not to say a word about tonight's little outing because, most likely, it was going to be a fool's errand.

Miss Claire was in that casket. Longarm had seen her in the park struck down by an assassin's deadly bullets.

Chapter 9

Longarm didn't really feel like leaving his apartment and going out to the Eternal Rest Cemetery. Most likely Wilbur Riley was just another wild kid with an overactive imagination. Still, he had to be certain so he left his apartment at sundown and caught a carriage. When he arrived at the cemetery it was in full darkness and the driver was obviously reluctant to enter the wrought iron gates.

"This is as far as I care to go," he told Longarm. "Do you want me to wait for you?"

"Yes," Longarm said. "I shouldn't be more than a half hour."

"I'll have to charge you an extra two bits for the wait."

"That will be fine," Longarm said, leaving the coach and starting into the cemetery.

"Be careful in there!" the driver shouted.

"I will."

Longarm cussed himself for forgetting to bring a lantern. Fortunately, the moon was up and there was enough glow from the city lamps to allow him a measure of visibility.

"Wilbur!" he shouted.

A light flickered some hundred yards off to his left. Then Longarm saw that it was Wilbur holding a match to his face. The match flickered and died, but not before Longarm had seen the path he would take through the graveyard.

"Thank God you came!" the boy whispered. "I got here in the daylight and it was bad enough then, but it's far worse now. This place is really spooky. My flesh is crawling like worms."

"Well," Longarm said, looking at Lilly's fresh grave piled with already wilting flowers, "it's not my favorite hangout, either. Did you bring a shovel?"

"Yes, sir."

"Then have at it, Wilbur."

Even in the moonlight Longarm saw the kid's face pale. "*I've* got to dig her up?"

"I can't," Longarm said, "because of my injuries. And besides, you need to earn your money. And you aren't *digging her up*, you're just exposing the casket. Big difference."

Wilbur wasn't persuaded. "Marshal, I'd as soon forget this whole creepy business."

"Dig," Longarm ordered.

Wilbur gulped and moved closer to the grave. "I've got to remove all these flowers first. I'm going to make a mess of this gravesite for certain."

"Miss Claire, if that's who's down there, won't mind at all," Longarm told him. "Now stop talking and start digging. I'm as anxious to get out of here as you are."

"I don't believe that," Wilbur said, tossing the flowers in every direction and then grabbing an old shovel he'd brought.

Longarm sat and leaned back against the headstone of a nearby grave. He poked a cigar into his mouth and

70

chewed on it thoughtfully. "You're doing pretty good there, Wilbur. Ever think of becoming a grave digger? You'd always have work."

"Hell, no! And the reason I'm going along so fast is that the ground is soft and I want to get out of here!"

"Don't strain your back," Longarm advised. "We'll see who's in that casket soon enough."

He was right. It took less than fifteen minutes of earnest dirt slinging before Wilbur struck the top of the casket. "Don't want to dent or scratch it up," the boy said. "It was real pretty."

"Miss Lilly won't mind."

Longarm climbed to his feet and went over to the side of the hole. "Just get that dirt cleaned off and let's get the thing open."

"Sir, I really don't want to do this!"

"Do it anyway."

"I done all the digging," Wilbur said, his voice begging. "Couldn't you at least be the one who opens the casket?"

Longarm could see that the kid was extremely upset, so he nodded and climbed down into the grave. "Give me the shovel and get back up there. I'll finish it off."

"Oh, thank you, sir!"

"That's all right," Longarm said, taking the shovel and setting to work.

It took another five minutes to get the dirt cleared away enough to open the casket. Longarm tossed the shovel up to Wilbur, lit a match and took a deep breath. "All right, here goes."

He lifted the lid with one hand and lowered the match with the other. Inside, he saw a woman who looked like Lilly Claire. She had the same long, black, lustrous hair, but was definitely someone else and not nearly as attractive.

The match burned the tips of his fingers and then died.

71

"What?" Wilbur asked.

"You were right. It's not Lilly Claire."

Wilbur let out an audible sigh. "Are you sure?"

"I am," Longarm answered. "But I just don't understand it. Come down here and hold this lid up while I check the body."

"No, sir!"

"Wilbur, dammit, you heard me. I need to look for wounds."

"Oh, no. I couldn't do that. Please!"

"Get down here!" Longarm snapped. "Do you think I'm enjoying this?"

"But it's your job, Marshal. It ain't mine."

"I'll pay you another five dollars."

Wilbur shook like a leaf in a high wind, but he jumped down into the grave to grab the lid. Longarm took a deep breath and lit a match. He bent over the body which was already beginning to putrefy. What he wanted to see was the exact placement of the bullet wounds. He had to know if they matched those that he had seen inflicted at the park.

Longarm's inspection took only moments before he was satisfied that this was the young woman who had been shot before his eyes only an instant after he had been seriously wounded.

"I thought Lilly had done a great job disguising herself," Longarm said more to himself than to the kid. "Fact is she didn't disguise herself at all. She switched persons with someone about her own age and size. But someone who was just a poor working girl. I don't know who this is but she wasn't Lilly Claire."

"Oh gawd, she really stinks!" Wilbur gagged. "Can I close the lid and then we can cover her up again?"

"Yes," Longarm said. "Do that."

He climbed out of the grave and was amazed at how

fast Wilbur covered the casket and rebuilt the mound. Longarm couldn't imagine who had been buried in this grave much less why. And as to the whereabouts of Lilly, he hadn't a clue. But one thing was for sure, when he found the famous singer, she'd have a lot of explaining to do.

"Now the flowers," Longarm said. "Put them neatly over the mound and let's be out of here."

"You got that right," Wilbur said, his face drenched with sweat although the night was cool.

Longarm and Wilbur hurried out of the graveyard, but when they got to the gate, the carriage was gone.

"Damn," Longarm swore. "He left."

"We can walk back to the city. I don't mind walking. Do you, Marshal?"

"Ordinarily I don't," Longarm told him, "but I'm not quite up to snuff this evening. Wilbur, someone has done a foul act for reasons I cannot yet understand and may never understand. And just because the woman in that casket isn't Miss Lilly, it doesn't make it any less of a case of murder."

"Yes, sir."

Longarm lit a cigar. "And you must never reveal what we found here tonight. If you do, your own life could be in danger."

"You mean . . ."

"I mean someone set this girl up to be murdered so that Miss Claire and Edward could disappear. Or maybe they sent this poor girl as a decoy and then fled assuming everyone—especially the man who is threatening her—would think that Lilly was dead."

"It's kind of confusing. Do you think that Miss Claire is behind this foul trickery?"

"Quite possibly. I don't know," Longarm admitted. "All that I am sure of is that if you were to say anything and it got back to them, they might well track you down and kill you. After all, up to tonight, you are the only witness to have seen the real Miss Claire alive."

"I'd as soon you paid me and then I'll be leaving."

"Where to?"

"Back to my city places, sir. I know how to hide from someone who is after me."

Longarm wondered what that meant but said, "Wilbur, I don't think that would be such a good idea."

"But it's the only place I can go. I have some friends I run with."

"I'm sure that you do." Longarm thought a moment. "Why don't you come and stay at my apartment for the next few days? You can sleep on my couch and I'll buy food to cook in my kitchen, small as it is."

"You really think my life is in that much danger?"

"I don't know yet," Longarm told the orphan, "but why take chances? Until I get some answers about why this deception has taken place, I see no need to risk your life."

Wilbur thought this over for a few moments and then said, "Can I have my money now?"

Longarm paid him. "Whether you come to my apartment and hide there or not is your choice."

"I'll come and stay with you for a day or two," Wilbur decided. "If you think that is best."

"I do."

"But, Marshal, I've got some things that I have to do first."

"What things?"

"Personal things," Wilbur said vaguely, his eyes drifting away. "Tell me where you live and I'll come by your place later tonight."

Longarm wasn't too happy with that, but he had no choice. Wilbur was wild and undisciplined. He wasn't ac-

74

customed to being told what to do and Longarm sensed that the kid wouldn't be pressured.

"All right. Knock twice, then wait a few seconds and knock twice more. I'll know for certain that it's you and I'll open the door."

"You're not a very trusting person."

"I can't afford to be," Longarm replied. "I've made too many enemies among bad people in this town."

"Okay," Wilbur said. "I'll see you later tonight."

"Don't tell anybody what we learned," Longarm warned. "Not a soul. Your life might depend on how well you can keep that secret."

"Fair enough."

Wilbur folded his money up neatly and stuffed it deep into his pockets. Then, with his head down he disappeared into the darkness, making his own secret way back into the city.

Chapter 10

Longarm decided that he had no choice but to go to see his boss early the next morning. He had a dozen different theories as to why Lilly Claire's funeral had been staged. But theories were just theories, nothing more and certainly not enough to hang a lawman's career upon. What he needed was to bring Billy into the picture and then let his boss decide their next course of action. After all, that was what Billy was being paid well to do . . . make the tough decisions.

Longarm was preparing to go to bed when there was a soft knock on his door. It couldn't be Wilbur Riley because he wasn't using the code. "Who is it?"

When no one answered his call, Longarm removed his gun from his holster and crept over to the locked door wearing nothing but a pair of shorts.

"I said, who is it?"

"My name is Sara. Miss Sara Lancaster. I work at the Birdcage Theater. You've seen me many times. I need to talk to you right now."

Longarm tried to recall Sara but failed. "Step back away from my door and keep your hands in plain sight," he ordered because there might be a man waiting beside Sara hoping to shoot him down.

"All right."

Longarm unlocked his door and eased it open with his pistol pointed out through the crack. He saw a young woman about twenty-five standing in the hallway. She was tall with long brown hair and a frightened look on her face. Longarm recognized Sara as one of the theater employees. She was a quiet and attractive young woman with a quick smile and friendly brown eyes.

"I'm not properly dressed," Longarm said, "and the hour grows late. Sara, what do you want?"

Sara gulped hard. "What I have to tell you is very troubling. And I'd rather not do it standing out here in the hallway."

"All right," Longarm said. "Give me a moment to dress."

He closed the door and locked it, then dressed. When he returned to the door the gun was still in his fist although now uncocked. He looked up and down the hallway, then said, "Come on inside."

"Thank you."

The moment the woman was inside, she whirled on Longarm and blurted, "That person in the casket is *not* Miss Claire!"

Longarm motioned for the clearly distraught woman to have a seat and then he placed his gun on his bedside table and sat down across from her. Not wanting to tip his own hand, he asked, "What makes you say that?"

"Because I'm sure that I saw Miss Claire and her half brother Edward just this afternoon." Sara bent forward, clasped her hands tightly together then shook her head in bewilderment. "Either that, or I'm going daft."

"*Where* did you think you saw her?"

"Exiting her apartment. You see, I rent a room only a block away. And as I was leaving to come to the theater, I saw a handsome young couple dart out of a brownstone and fly into a carriage. The man had a very tight grip on the woman's arm. He was pushing her and she was resisting. But, quick as you please, the carriage pulled away. By then, I was so certain that it was Miss Claire and her brother that I cried out for them to stop."

"But they didn't?"

"No," Sara said, confusion plain on her face, "but Lilly did turn toward the sound of my voice. That's when I was certain that I hadn't been mistaken."

"How far were you from them?" Longarm asked.

"Not far. Fifty feet."

"Had Miss Claire's appearance changed?"

Sara nodded. "That's what threw me off at first. This woman had blond hair. Also, she was wearing an old black dress. The kind you would wear if you were poor and going to a funeral. Also, I think she was barefoot."

"That is strange," Longarm said. "She could have been wearing a blond wig. But I still don't understand how can you be sure that it wasn't a woman who merely resembled Lilly."

"I wouldn't be so sure it was Miss Claire except that she turned to me at that moment in the carriage just as it was leaving. When she did her eyes were wide with fear. And she mouthed a word meant only for me."

"A word?"

"Yes," Sara said, "a single word."

"Do you have any idea . . ."

"I do," Sara interrupted. "Miss Claire had silently cried *help!*"

Longarm shook his head even though his heart was beginning to beat faster with excitement. "Sara," he began, "what you are saying is pretty hard to believe. I mean, at fifty feet you can read a single word?"

"I can read lips as well as anyone," she told him. "My father and mother were both deaf. Would you like me to read your lips? If you don't believe me, tell me something without the sound."

"All right."

Longarm silently told her she was right, that she probably had seen Lilly.

"Then you *do* believe me!" the woman cried with relief.

"Yes," Longarm said.

"But how can this be when we were both at Miss Claire's funeral?"

Longarm didn't really want to tell anyone what he and Wilbur Riley had discovered so he sidestepped the question. "I would like you to take me to the place where Miss Claire lived."

"Tonight?"

"Yes," he said, "it's very important that we do that now. And by the way, did Edward live with her?"

"I don't know. I'm pretty sure that they lived in the same building."

"All right," Longarm said, pulling on his boots and reaching for his gun belt. "Let's go."

When they reached the apartment Miss Claire and Edward had been seen leaving earlier, Sara stood back as Longarm knocked on the landlord's door. An old woman in a shabby nightgown and shawl finally opened the door and she wasn't happy.

"Dammit, who are you and what do you want?" she cried, spittle flying.

Longarm showed her his badge and requested to see Lilly's apartment. The old woman growled and cussed, but she had no choice but to lead them to Lilly's door.

Once inside the apartment, Longarm did a quick inspection. In the closets, he found men and women's clothing that he recognized as belonging to both Lilly and Edward. He searched for correspondence and found a discarded envelope, but no accompanying letter.

"Where was the letter posted?" Sara asked.

Longarm held it up to a kerosene lamp he'd lighted. "Looks like it's postmarked in Salt Lake City."

He searched again but could not find the accompanying letter or anything else that would give any indication of Lilly or Edward's shadowy past.

"I recognize most of her dresses," Sara said, poking around in the closet. "Do you think she is ever returning for them?"

"I wouldn't bet on it," Longarm replied.

Sara sat down on the bed. "I don't understand any of this. If Miss Claire is not dead and that wasn't her resting in the casket, then who . . ."

"I don't know," Longarm said, "but it's a strange and dark mystery. One I intend to solve."

"Do you think Miss Claire is all right?"

"No," Longarm answered, "and from your description of her as she was being pulled into that carriage, I'm sure you don't think that Miss Claire was safe, either."

"I certainly don't," Sara said. "I never did like Edward. I'm an only child and I've always wanted sisters and brothers, but not one like him. There was something wrong with the man. Something scary."

"I'm sure that he wasn't actually her brother," Longarm said, putting his unspoken thoughts into words. "Edward was probably Lilly's lover . . . or even her secret husband. I don't know. Maybe he was all three."

"A lover who was a brother!" Sara cried, clearly appalled. "I can't believe that. It's . . . it's depraved."

"You find it hard to believe because you haven't seen the darker side of life."

"Marshal, I'm no blushing virgin or high society flower," she told him. "I've been around and not much surprises me anymore when it comes to what people are capable of doing to each other. You should understand that there are a lot of strange people who work at the Birdcage Theater. Strange, intensely ambitious and not always so nice beneath their smiling surface."

Longarm imagined this was probably true. "I've seen enough here. Let's get out of this place."

"But you have no idea where they went?"

Longarm consulted his watch. "The train heading up to Cheyenne left late this afternoon. My bet is that they boarded it."

"On their way to Salt Lake City?"

"Maybe, but they could have headed east," he said. "I'll talk to the conductor and ticket master and attempt to find out where they went after they arrived at Cheyenne."

"What if they used aliases?"

"They probably did," Longarm said. "But Lilly is so striking that she would almost certainly be remembered even wearing an old black dress."

"Yes," Sara said, "I'm sure you're right. Are you going to the train depot right now?"

"I am." Longarm was already leaving.

"Marshal, I'd like to come along."

"What for?"

Sara raised her hands then dropped them helplessly at

her sides. "I just don't feel safe. I feel like I saw something outside that I shouldn't have and that I'm in danger."

"I doubt that is true."

"But it *could* be true."

Longarm could see that she was genuinely worried. He also realized that it wasn't fair to just abandon Sara after all the help she'd given him. "Yes," he admitted. "I suppose it could be true that you are in some danger."

"Then I'd feel better staying with you tonight."

He didn't know what to say about that so he just headed for the door. As they passed outside the landlady stuck her head out into the hallway and screamed, "You have no right to come snoopin' around at this hour! No right to rob an old woman of her precious sleep!"

"Sorry," Longarm called back over his shoulder as he took the stairs two at a time and Sara tried to keep up.

A short time later, Longarm and Sara were at the train depot. They found the place deserted except for a porter who was stacking some boxes and filling out paperwork.

"Yeah, Marshal, I remember 'em," he said. "Especially the woman. I overheard the man talking with her when he bought them tickets to Cheyenne. The blond woman was a looker but she acted nervous and maybe even frightened. The man who bought the tickets was in a hurry and wasn't being very nice to the lady. Not nice at all."

"What do you mean?"

"When the train was ready to go, he practically dragged her on board. The woman burst into tears. Me and a lot of other men watching what was going on were pretty angry about that man's brutish behavior."

The porter sighed and shook his head with regret. "Maybe I should have had a firm word with the man but he looked like trouble from the top of his hat to the toes of his shoes. And I don't need trouble, Marshal. I got a wife and kids to feed. I'm no fighter. He was a lot bigger 'n me and stronger, too. So I held my tongue, but I was angry."

"Did you overhear the man say anything about where they were going after they reached Cheyenne?"

"No, sir. But he was in a big hurry to leave Denver. He was a real shit-head, that one. Pushin' his pretty wife around so hard. I could tell I wasn't the only one that didn't like him. There were a lot of other men who looked like they was about to try and help the woman. But the man looked dangerous. He looked like the kind that would kill you if you crossed him."

Longarm asked a few more questions but didn't learn much. "Does the train still leave just once a day?"

"Yep. Four-ten tomorrow afternoon."

"Thanks," Longarm said. "I expect I'll be on it."

"You chasing that bully, are you?"

"Yes."

"For hurting someone?"

"I think so."

The porter's eyes took on an excitement. "Killin' someone even?"

"I can't say because it's official business," Longarm replied. "Thanks for your information."

"You got a pretty woman, too," the porter said, smiling for the first time and looking at Sara. He winked. "Seems like a real sweet and juicy young tomato."

Longarm would have laughed if the situation had not been so grim.

Chapter 11

Longarm had planned to escort Sara to her apartment but she didn't want to be alone. "I could be in real danger, couldn't I?"

"It's unlikely," he told the young woman. "But I'm not prepared to rule it out entirely."

"What if I came to your apartment and spent the night. You know, sleep on the couch?"

"I don't have a couch."

"Well, then on the floor."

"Really, I doubt that it is necessary."

"Please," she said, "I'd feel much safer."

Longarm was a gentleman and a gentleman never refused the request of a lady and Sara was genuinely frightened.

"I have a young man named Wilbur Riley coming up to my apartment. He is also in some danger."

"Who is he?"

"He's a fifteen-year-old street kid. I'm trying to help him out."

"Well," Sara said, "if you don't mind, my motto has always been the more the merrier."

Longarm took Sara by the arm. "Come along then."

When they got to his apartment, there was a note slipped under the door. It was poorly written and from Wilbur explaining that he had changed his mind and decided to take his chances on the street among friends.

"He's not coming?" Sara asked, seeing the frown on Longarm's face.

"That's right."

"Are you disappointed?"

"Frankly, I am. I liked the kid and had thought I might be able to help him out in some small way. Perhaps find a family for young Wilbur to live with. Some nice people who would give him a roof over his head. He could also use a father figure to give him some direction in his life."

"You're a Good Samaritan," Sara told him. "You take in and protect the frightened and the lonely souls of Denver."

"Are you a lonely soul?" Longarm asked.

"Sort of," Sara admitted. "I didn't want to tell you this but I'm also a broke, unemployed and homeless soul."

"What about your job at the theater?"

"When the news hit town that Miss Claire had been murdered, everything fell apart at work. The next performance was canceled and we were all told not to report to work until the owner figured out what he wanted to do next. Frankly, I think that he lost money paying Miss Claire so much for such a short stage appearance. The crowds that came to see her were good, but not good enough to offset all the overhead. The truth is, Miss Claire's engagement was a financial disaster, according to the theater owner."

"I'm both sorry and surprised to hear that."

"And," Sara continued, "Miss Claire and Edward borrowed funds that were not repaid."

Longarm frowned as he unlocked his door and they entered his apartment. "Are you suggesting that Miss Claire was in financial difficulties?"

"I don't know," Sara replied. "But I think it is possible."

Longarm closed the door and unbuckled his gun belt. "Would you like a drink?" he offered. "All I have is whiskey and water."

"I'll have both. Where is the toilet?"

"Go out into the hall and turn left. It's at the end and marked."

"I'll be right back," Sara told him. "Pour me a stiff one. This has been quite an unsettling evening."

Longarm poured them both three fingers of good Kentucky whiskey. He added a little water to Sara's glass but drank his straight. When the young woman returned, she was carrying her underclothes and shoes, wearing only her dress and blouse.

When Longarm gave her a quizzical glance, she explained. "I want to sleep comfortably as I can on your floor."

"Listen," Longarm said, already feeling guilty, "you can sleep on my bed. I'll sleep on the floor."

Sara would have nothing of it. "No. You were good enough to let me come up here tonight and I don't want to impose."

Longarm was in no mood to argue. Sara could sleep on the floor, if she insisted. He gave her the whiskey and water asking, "What are you going to do without a job and no money?"

"I have a little savings," she confessed. "Just not enough to pay the rent and buy food until I find new employment."

Without hesitation Longarm said, "Sara, if you'd like, you can stay here. I'm leaving tomorrow and there is no telling when I'll return. My rent is paid up until the end of the month and someone might as well take advantage of that fact. Besides, there's this old black cat that shows up at the window. I feed him because I think he's not up to hunting anymore. I'd like you to see that he doesn't go hungry while I'm gone."

"I love cats! Is he wild, or can I pet him?"

"That will be up to Midnight," Longarm said. "He takes a big liking to some people but he can't abide others. I expect he will warm to you in a hurry if you feed and talk to him. I leave my window open a crack so that he can come and go as he pleases. I don't like to think of the old boy shivering outside in bad weather."

"I'll be happy to take care of Midnight." Sara threw her arms around Longarm. "So while you're gone, I'll feed the cat and look for another job. Something more stable than the theater, although I love that atmosphere. I always wanted to be an actress, you know. But I'm not pretty or talented like Lilly Claire. I realize that now but I still love the theater."

"Never give up on your dreams. And I sure don't agree that you're not pretty enough to be on stage. I think you're very attractive."

"Really?" Sara beamed. "You're not just saying that?"

"No. I mean it."

Sara must not have been accustomed to receiving compliments because she beamed at his words. "Do you have a sweetheart, Marshal Long?"

"Nope."

"But you were sweet on Miss Claire. Everyone who meets her is soon smitten."

Longarm shrugged. "I won't lie and tell you that I

didn't find her very attractive. But I'm sure not heartbroken because she's out of my life. I'm just wondering why she's gone and who's buried in her casket. That's what is driving me crazy."

"Yes," Sara said. "Did you actually see the corpse?"

"Wilbur Riley and I went to the cemetery and opened the casket. The woman inside bore only the faintest resemblance to Miss Claire. There is not a doubt in my mind that she was a victim of some foul and despicable treachery. And tomorrow when I go to my office, I will tell my boss and Billy will almost certainly have the body exhumed."

Sara shook her head. "If the newspapers get wind of that, there will be quite a stir."

"I'm hoping that Billy Vail can keep the whole thing under wraps until we find out who that poor woman was and why she was murdered."

"I can understand that." Sara kissed Longarm. "Let's talk about something nicer. Do you really think I'm pretty and desirable?"

"Sure do."

"And do I *have* to sleep on your floor tonight?"

"Not if you don't want to."

"What do *you* want me to do?"

Longarm's mind had been so preoccupied by the mystery of Lilly Claire's disappearance that he hadn't even thought about lovemaking with Sara. But she was rubbing her hips against his hips and he could feel nothing but luscious flesh under her blouse.

"Let's go to bed," he told her. "And see what happens."

Sara giggled and blushed. "I'm pretty sure what's going to happen."

"Me, too."

Longarm undressed quickly and turned down the lamp.

Sara managed to get naked even faster and when he came down on her, she was hot, wet and ready. He entered her and she sighed with pleasure.

"You more than fill me up," she whispered. "Custis, you're hung like a donkey!"

"How do you know how a donkey is hung?"

"Really big. You see, I've seen them in action. A big donkey mounting a mare is something a girl doesn't quickly forget."

Longarm began to stir Sara. "And is this what watching that jack made you think about?"

"It sure is!" Sara wrapped her legs around Longarm and locked her heels at his spine. "Do it to me, Marshal. Poke me deep and strong. But don't rush it, okay? I want this to last and I won't be satisfied until we're both bucking and howling with pleasure!"

Just then, the old black stray, Midnight, jumped through the window and let out a pitiful howl.

"Get lost!" Longarm warned.

But the black cat was starving and insistent. He jumped up on the bed next to Sara and Longarm. He sniffed at their sex and howled even louder.

"Maybe he remembers his best days when he was tom-catting around," Sara said, trying not to laugh. "Maybe our smell makes him sad."

"I don't give a damn what it makes him feel like," Longarm said, wanting to get back to the joy of their lovemaking. "Midnight, I'm going to wring your scrawny neck if you don't get off this bed."

He took a swipe at the old alley cat but Midnight was still quick enough to dodge and escape. Longarm wished he'd have shot back out through the window but he jumped up on the kitchen table and continued to howl.

"Let's give him something to eat," Sara said. "He looks so thin and scroungy."

"Why don't we just forget the damned cat," Longarm growled, shoving his tool as deep as he could into Sara and trying to get back into the flow of their lovemaking.

"Please," she whispered. "We've got all night to do this."

"And he's got all night to eat."

"I can't do this with Midnight howling so pitifully. Couldn't you just give him something to eat. Or some warm milk."

"Midnight never drinks milk. He takes water and meat."

"Then feed the poor cat and come back to me."

Longarm could see that he had no choice. Biting back a few choice cuss words, he jumped off the delicious young woman, raced to his icebox and found the cat some meat. He tossed about a quarter pound of lean beef to Midnight who pounced on it and began to eat like he was having his last meal.

"There," Longarm said. "Are you satisfied?"

"Give him something to drink, too."

"Shit!"

Longarm gave the stray water and then he rushed back to Sara who opened herself and gave him a big smile. "You do have such a good and generous heart. And don't worry about Midnight while you're gone. I'll love him and take good care of the old boy."

"Let's forget about the damned cat," Longarm growled as he plunged his rod back into Sara.

"Don't rush," she begged. "Please don't rush this."

"Midnight eats fast."

Sara giggled until Longarm got to her again, causing

her to moan with pleasure. "You're a monster at lovemaking," Sara cried. "I knew you would be!"

"How did you know that?" he asked, not really caring but enjoying himself immensely as he hitched her thighs up high in order to drive even deeper into her sweet honey pot.

"I just knew," she panted, forcing his head down between her heaving breasts. "Suck them. Oh, this is nice!"

Longarm stirred the young woman until she howled with joy.

Finally, Sara cried, "Oh my god, I'm going out of my mind. Take me now, Marshal!"

Longarm obliged. He felt his body convulse as he shot his seed into Sara who began to buck. Over by the kitchen, Midnight finished his meat and began to howl along with the woman.

All in all, they were making one hell of a racket and he was glad that he was making everyone happy . . . including himself.

"Look at that old cat," Sara said, a few minutes later as they were trying to regain their breath. "He's sniffing my underpants."

"He is definitely remembering his younger days," Longarm said. "The old lecher."

"I really like him," Sara told him. "He's so ugly that he's cute."

"He likes you, too," Longarm added. "Look at the way his upper lip is curling as he sniffs your undergarments. If I were you, I'd be careful when he's in the room with you at night."

Sara laughed and poked Longarm in the ribs hard. "Don't you worry about it," she said. "He can't have a ding dong any bigger than my little finger."

"You may discover differently."

Sara dug her thumb into Longarm again and then she snuggled close to him and whispered, "I'm going to miss you. So will Midnight. So please take care of yourself and come back whole and safe. For our sakes as well as your own."

"I'll do my level best," Longarm promised. "Are you ready for some sleep?"

"No. I'm ready for more of you inside of me."

"That sounds good to me," Longarm replied, feeling better than he had all day and glad to have his mind off the feigned murder and disappearance of Lilly Claire. He still had no idea what was going on, but he was sure it was bad news. Maybe that Edward fella had already killed Lilly and tossed her body off on the side of the railroad tracks.

There was just no way of telling. All he knew for certain was that he had to find that woman in order to save her life. And he had to do it in a big hurry starting tomorrow.

Chapter 12

Longarm left Sara and Midnight the next morning feeling as if he'd been pulled through the wringer. He hadn't gotten much sleep the night before and he was feeling a touch light-headed. But he was smiling. Sara was going to spend the morning moving things from her apartment over to his apartment. "And when you get back, you'll hardly recognize the place," she had vowed. "I'm going to fix it up real nice."

Longarm caught an image of doilies and lace and it didn't sit well. "Look," he said, "don't do much. I like things simple. Besides, you need to find a job and save enough money to get a place of your own. Remember?"

She kissed his mouth. "Do you really want me to move out as soon as I can?"

He didn't quite know what to say. "Just . . . just enjoy yourself and watch out for my alley cat."

"Will do."

Midnight had vanished sometime in the wee hours of the morning, but Longarm knew the cat would return soon for another meal. Hell, by the time he returned from Salt

Lake City or wherever the path would lead in this investigation, Midnight would probably be domesticated.

And that would be a pity.

When Longarm arrived at the federal building, he went straight to his boss's office but Billy's secretary stopped him at the door.

"Mr. Vail hasn't arrived yet."

Longarm consulted his pocket watch. "It's nine-fifteen. He's usually here by eight. What's up?"

"I have no idea. But he'll be in soon. You know Billy. He'd come in even if he had to climb off his deathbed."

"Yeah, I guess you're right."

Longarm found himself a cup of strong coffee, blew the steam off it and went to his desk. Some of the other staff were milling about, but it being Monday morning, no one was talking much.

"Well as I live and breathe!" Marshal Dan Hooker exclaimed, sauntering into the room. "Look what the cat drug in this morning!"

Longarm glanced up at the loudmouth and said, "Shut up, Dan. I'm in no mood for your bullshit."

Hooker scoffed and tried to look as if his feelings had been injured. "What's the matter, Marshal Long? Did you have your usual dissipated night? Or maybe you couldn't get it up and your latest whore explained what a loser you really are."

Longarm looked up at the man who was smirking. "I'm givin' you a chance to drag your big ass outta here, Dan. You'd be smart to take it."

But Hooker had no intention of leaving. He was having fun and playing to an audience of his fellow office workers and lawmen. "Aw, you sound real bad this morning,

Custis. I'm sorry about whatever it is that got you down. But life is tough. You're just going to have to . . ."

Longarm's coffee was so hot that he had barely taken a sip. He studied Hooker, then his coffee and decided that the two should get acquainted. "You had your coffee yet?" he asked pleasantly.

Dan was surprised by the question but then recovered. "No, I was just about to get a cup."

"Don't bother," Longarm said, hurling his steaming cup of coffee into the big marshal's face.

Dan Hooker let out a bellow that could have been heard along Cherry Creek. He covered his face and that's when Longarm eased out of his office chair and punched the man. It was a short, powerful uppercut to the brisket and it doubled up Hooker. While the man was still blinded and in serious pain, Longarm shot a straight left to the man's jaw that bowled him over a nearby desk.

"Oh, boy!" another marshal shouted. "We got some excitement around here! Everybody step back and give 'em some room!"

Longarm could have gone over and kicked Hooker in the head thus ending the fight in a hurry, but he didn't. Instead, he waited for the man to come to his feet and dry his eyes.

Hooker's face was beet red and he was swearing a blue streak. "I'm going to dish your hash! I'm going to beat your ass!"

"Come along then," Longarm said, wiping a couple of scraped and bleeding knuckles on his pants. "This has been building for a long time and I think we ought to settle it once and for all."

Hooker charged with his mighty arms swinging. He outweighed Longarm by a good thirty pounds and had the

97

advantage in brute strength. But he wasn't fast nor was he skilled. Most likely, his imposing size and strength had intimidated most adversaries and so he was lacking real fighting experience.

Longarm ducked a roundhouse right and shot his own right to the man's watery eye. Hooker rocked back blinking tears. The eye would close quickly and Longarm decided it needed an identical match so he dodged, blocked a punch and poked a stiff left into Hooker's other eye.

"Stand still and fight like a man!" Hooker bellowed as a crowd gathered to cheer them on and Hooker tried to wipe the tears from his eyes and clear his watery vision.

"All right, come on and get it, big man."

Hooker came in again but more cautiously this time. He feinted with a left, threw a hard right and then took a hard punch in retaliation but still managed to muscle Longarm into a wall. Now sensing he had the advantage, Hooker slammed his forehead into Longarm's face, trying to break his nose. Longarm managed to turn and take the stunning blow on his cheekbone. His head bounced off the wall and he felt Hooker pound him with two thundering body shots.

Longarm knew that he had to get off the wall. He twisted and when that didn't work, he hooked a leg behind Hooker and then threw his shoulder into the man causing him to lose his balance. Free at last, Longarm spun around and drove a furious volley of punches into Hooker's body. The man tried to grab Longarm and break his ribs but failed.

Longarm stepped back feeling as if he'd been kicked in the sides by a horse. But at least Hooker's eyes were red and still filled with tears. Even more encouraging was the fact that they were swelling shut fast.

"Had enough?" Longarm asked.

"Hell, no!"

"Then you're even dumber than I thought," Longarm said, throwing caution to the wind and wading in with fists flying.

Hooker was against the wall now and he tried to fight his way out of it but Longarm didn't give him that opportunity. He hit the man in the body repeatedly with all the strength he owned, and when Hooker tried to cover up there, Longarm changed his attack and smashed at Hooker's face until it was pulpy. He detested the man and meant to beat him so badly that he would never mouth off again or badger anyone else at work.

"He's finished!" a woman cried. "Custis, please stop or you're going to kill him!"

But Longarm's blood was up and he wasn't going to quit until Hooker was lying flat on the floor.

Finally the big man slid down the wall covering his face and begging for mercy. It was a pitiful sight and that's when Longarm let others in the office pull him back.

"Dan, if you ever taunt me or anyone else again around here I swear I'll kill you with my own hands," Longarm vowed, fists still clenched.

"Custis!"

Longarm dropped his fists and turned around knowing that Billy Vail had arrived.

"What the hell is going on here?" his boss demanded.

"Dan Hooker and I have come to a little understanding." Longarm slowly turned to Hooker whose eyes were now closed into tight red slits. "Isn't that right, Dan?"

All Hooker could do was nod his head in agreement.

Longarm wiped his bloody knuckles on his pants again and went over to the coffeepot. He refilled his cup, then walked back to his desk.

Billy Vail stalked him. "Custis?"

"Yes, sir?"

"What in God's name have you done to Hooker?"

Longarm blew steam off his fresh cup and looked at the man he had worked for over the years. "Billy, I've just established a new working relationship between Hooker and the rest of your office. One that I think will be much improved, morale wise."

Vail began to sneeze. When the sneezing ended, he blew his nose and muttered, "I've got a temperature of one hundred and four degrees and my head feels like it is packed with cement. I'm ready to die, but I still dragged myself into the office. And what do I find? One of my deputy marshals beating the hell out of another deputy marshal!"

"I can promise that it won't happen again," Longarm said, sipping his coffee. "Will it, Dan?"

Dan said something through his broken lips nobody in the office could understand.

"Dan said it won't happen again," Longarm told his boss. "We've got it all settled. I'm sorry you're feeling so bad, boss. But I've got some things that I have to talk over with you so I'm glad you did climb off your deathbed to come into work."

Billy opened his mouth to say something but thought better of it. He motioned Longarm inside his office and shouted, "Someone take Dan to the doctor before he bleeds to death!"

Longarm looked back at the thoroughly beaten man and then he surveyed his fellow workers and was rewarded with smiles.

"All right," Longarm said, turning and going into Billy's office. "Now just settle down and listen to me because what I have to say is going to be quite a shock . . . especially to a sick man."

"I'm already in shock. Close my damned door."

Longarm took a seat as far as possible from his boss because he didn't want to get whatever serious illness Billy had contracted.

Billy collapsed in his office chair. He looked terrible and sounded worse. "I could fire you, Custis. In fact, I *ought* to fire you and Dan both. What the hell kind of thing is that . . . getting into a brawl right here in the federal building! What kind of an example does this set? And can you imagine what people elsewhere in this building will be saying when they find out that you nearly killed a fellow lawman!"

"The trouble here was a long time coming," Longarm said calmly. "Maybe you weren't aware of it, but Marshal Hooker has been bullying some of your other men for years. Not physically pushing them around, maybe, but insulting them and making them feel small. It's something I thought you'd eventually see and take care of, but you didn't. So when he started taunting me first thing this morning, I decided to take care of it myself."

"You are way out of line," Billy said just before he broke out into another episode of sneezing. He grabbed for a handkerchief and lustily blew his nose.

"You really should be home in bed," Longarm told the man. "But first, I want to tell you that Lilly Claire isn't resting in her coffin."

Billy dropped both hands to his desk and stared.

"You heard me right." Longarm explained how he and Wilbur Riley had gone to the cemetery and exhumed the body. "I don't know who the woman was that we had the funeral for," he said in conclusion. "But, if I were you, I'd have the body examined and perhaps a portrait drawn of her face and that placed in the newspaper. It would help to get identification, although that might never be possible."

"So what happened to Miss Claire?" Billy had already completely forgotten about firing his favorite deputy marshal.

"She and Edward boarded a train yesterday bound for Cheyenne. For all I know they are long gone but I'm hoping they went to Salt Lake City."

When Billy asked Longarm why Utah, Longarm showed him the envelope with the all-important postmark. "I went to Miss Claire's apartment. She had obviously been living with Edward who is probably either her husband or her lover. Anyway, they were seen leaving in a carriage. Lilly was wearing a blond wig and she looked scared to death."

"Do you think Miss Claire is a murderer?"

"I hope not, but it's very possible."

Billy shook his head in bewilderment. "But why would a woman who has fame and fortune be a part of such a thing?"

"That's what I mean to find out . . . if you'll give me the time and some travel money."

Billy wiped his runny nose. "How much time and money?"

"As much as it takes. I'll get on the northbound this afternoon and start asking questions as soon as I reach Cheyenne. It's entirely possible that Lilly and Edward have gone east. In that case, the trail will be even more difficult to follow."

"Yes, it would be. Especially if Miss Claire remains in disguise."

"I expect that she will be."

Billy's head dropped down to his chest and he looked awful. "I'm not capable of coherent thought," he said.

"Go home and get to bed," Longarm ordered. "But first, sign the orders so that I can go after Lilly and Edward. And don't be cheap with the travel money. I may have to be gone for quite some time."

"We can't spare you for a long time. You've got two weeks."

"Impossible," Longarm replied. "Three is minimum. And I won't stay in fleabag hotels. I insist on traveling right."

"My budget is in bad shape. I can advance you two hundred dollars. That's the very best that I can do until you have some solid leads."

"Fair enough," Longarm told him. "I'm on my way."

Billy's fevered mind was drifting. "I just can't understand this," he said, staring into space. "Why on earth would a woman like that be involved in a murder?"

"Maybe it was a matter of insurance," Longarm replied. "Or perhaps she was forced to take part in this deceit. I'd like to think that the latter was the reason but I simply don't know. But I do mean to find out."

"Keep in touch," Billy said. "I'll expect frequent telegrams."

"Maybe I'll get lucky and catch up with them in Cheyenne."

"Not likely."

Longarm nodded, knowing this was true. Whatever else Lilly and Edward were, they weren't stupid. And that was why Longarm would bet his bottom dollar that the mysterious pair was already hundreds of miles away.

Chapter 13

Longarm boarded the northbound for Cheyenne and fell asleep the moment he gave his ticket to the conductor and took his seat. It was about a hundred miles up to Cheyenne and he figured that would get him about three hours of solid sleep.

"Marshal!"

Longarm awoke with a start. He glanced up at the conductor who had a worried expression on his face. "What's wrong?"

"We've got a problem up in the first-class coach," the conductor said.

"Then take care of it." Longarm looked out the window and recognized familiar landmarks. He was only halfway to Cheyenne and that meant he was only halfway through his badly needed sleep. "It's your job."

The conductor was in his sixties with silver hair and a drooping mustache. Longarm took this train so frequently that he even remembered the conductor's name which was Albert Weir.

"Marshal, a man in the first-class coach has gotten

drunk and turned violent. He has beaten his wife and abused their son. We've tried to talk to him but he's being wild and unreasonable."

Longarm sighed. "How bad is the wife?"

"Black eye and puffy lips. He punched her around pretty good before she managed to get away from him."

"Tell me about the boy."

"He's just a toddler but he understands something is wrong and is quite upset. We don't know what to do."

"Overpower the son of a bitch and tie him up."

"We'd do that except that the husband is waving a gun around. He's so drunk that it's hard to understand what set him off but I think his wife has threatened to leave him and take their son away."

"Good idea," Longarm drawled. "I've no use for a wife-beater. Albert, can't you just put the wife and boy into another compartment?"

"The husband won't let either of them out of his grasp. When my superior tried to disarm him, he was threatened with a bullet to the brain. Marshal Long, we have a real crisis. All the first-class passengers are in a panic. I was hoping that, if you showed him your badge . . . and given your size . . . you could . . ."

There was no way that Longarm could go back to sleep and ignore a situation like this. "All right, Albert, I'll see what I can do. Is his gun really loaded?"

"We assume it is. None of us wants to put it to the test."

Longarm rubbed the sleep from his eyes. "The train is going to owe me a ride next trip."

"We'll see to that, Marshal Long," Albert said with relief in his voice. "It won't be a problem, I promise."

"First class. Not back here in coach again."

Albert nodded. "I'm sure that can be managed. But

would you please hurry? This man looks capable of shooting both his wife and his little boy!"

Longarm stood up and involuntarily groaned with pain that emanated from his badly bruised ribs. Billy Vail had been right; he shouldn't have stooped so low as to get into a brawl with Marshal Hooker. Instead, he should have cleanly knocked the big mouth out cold with his gun barrel. If he'd done that, he wouldn't be wincing with pain.

"Please follow me," the conductor said.

Longarm grabbed the man by his sleeve. "Why don't you follow me," he said. "If I've got to take care of this guy, I'd rather not have you standing between us."

"Thank you," the conductor said, obviously filled with gratitude. "But be very careful. This man was already drunk when he boarded the train in Denver. And there's a look in his eye that tells me he is desperate and out of control."

"I understand," Longarm said.

On his way forward, Longarm felt a rising concern. A man so depraved that he would beat his wife in front of his own son was a man that was capable of any level of violence. Longarm was wearing his usual brown tweed suit and matching vest, a blue-gray shirt with a shoestring tie and a snuff-brown Stetson hat with the crown flat on top. In one pocket of his vest was a .44-caliber derringer attached to a gold chain and Ingersol pocket watch. More than once he had pretended to check the time by pulling out the watch but instead producing the deadly little pistol. If need be, he'd use the derringer on the man.

"I'll never understand a man who could threaten his wife and kid," Albert said as they hurried through the cars.

"Me, neither," Longarm replied. "Such men are usually capable of killing not only their families, but also themselves."

"I wish this crazy bastard would shoot himself and be done with it," the conductor said. "He's no good. Any man that would behave this way deserves to be planted six feet under the ground."

"Maybe so," Longarm said, "but I would very much prefer to let the law decide his fate. Is there a place where he can be secured in custody?"

"Yes, the mail room. You've handcuffs?"

"Unfortunately not," Longarm said. "We'll have to find some rope."

"To tie around his throat before we heave him off the train?"

"No, to keep him under control until we hand him over to the authorities in Cheyenne."

Albert said nothing more as they hurried through the railroad cars. Longarm met several first-class passengers who were fleeing their seats. Some of them tried to stop Longarm and the conductor but Longarm brushed them aside. From their expressions, he could see a great deal of fear.

"Here we are," the conductor said. "Once you open that door, I'd have my gun in my hand, Marshal."

Longarm hesitated for a moment, gathering his wits. "If I go in waving a gun, he might start shooting. His wife, little boy or other innocent passengers could be killed. That's why I'll try to talk him into surrendering."

"It won't work."

"If not, I'll do whatever it takes," Longarm said pushing the door open and barging inside.

He took in the scene with a glance. A pretty dark-haired woman was lying in the aisle weeping and bent over a toddler, her body acting as a shield. Passengers were stiff in their seats, expressions twisted by fear. A heavyset and well-dressed man with a gun in one hand and a bottle of whiskey in the other was standing in the aisle trying to keep from falling over as the train rocked from side to side.

"Put the gun down," Longarm said in his most reasonable tone of voice as he walked up the aisle. "And let's talk."

The drunk with the gun squinted and blinked. No doubt he was seeing double and trying to focus on this unexpected intruder. "Who the hell are you?" he demanded, waving his gun in a circle as if he were fending off flies.

"I'm a deputy United States marshal."

"No shit!"

"No shit," Longarm echoed, sizing up every aspect of the coach and assessing the difficulty of this situation.

"Lessee yer badge, Mr. Marshal."

Longarm showed it to the man. He glanced down at the woman huddled in the aisle trying to protect her son. Her face was swollen and bloody. Tears streaked her battered face and the child she was clutching was whimpering.

"Drop the gun," Longarm ordered, looking back at the sorry excuse for a husband and father. "Mister, you got way too drunk and now you've created more than enough trouble for one day."

The train passed through a gentle curve and the man had to set his bottle in the seat and steady himself. "Are you gonna try and arrest me, Marshal?"

"That's right."

Suddenly, the drunken fool giggled and pointed his gun at Longarm. "You wanta die right here and now, lawman?"

Longarm felt the hair on the back of his neck stand straight up. The gun barrel was shaking and waving, but the range between them was only about fifteen feet. Even seeing double the man was very likely to kill him with his first or second shot. "Take it easy. You're in trouble but not so much that you'll be sent to prison. Kill me or someone else on this train and you'll spend the rest of your days rotting behind bars. Is that what you want?"

The man blinked, gun still pointed at Longarm's chest. "I ain't never ever going to prison! And I ain't gonna let her take my son from me just because I slapped her around a few times."

"A few times?" He tried to keep the anger from showing in his voice. "I'll bet you've slapped her around a lot," Longarm spat. "Why don't you drop that gun and try to slap *me* around? Or are you only man enough to beat up women and frighten little children?"

The drunk's eyes blazed with hatred. "You git out of here right now! Git or I'll put a bullet in your head!"

Longarm swore he could see the man's finger tightening on the trigger. "All right," he said, throwing his hands up. "Take it easy and don't shoot."

The drunk laughed and it wasn't a nice sound. "Are you pissin' your pants, Marshal? Have you got yellow water runnin' into your boots?"

Longarm had made up his mind what he had to do next. "That's right. How'd you guess."

"And you say I'm not a man? Ha! You're a coward!"

Longarm began to back toward the rear of the coach. He reached behind him and slowly opened the door. The woman on the floor stared at him and then began to wail hysterically as he inched out of the first class and then closed the door behind him with the drunk laughing crazily.

Albert was waiting between the cars, and when Longarm appeared he shouted over the noisy clanking of the railroad tracks. "Marshal Long, what happened in there?"

Longarm drew a deep breath of fresh air and unholstered the Colt revolver that he carried on his left hip, butt forward. "You were right, Albert. The man just won't listen to reason and he's plenty willing to die so long as he can take someone with him."

Albert stared at the gun in Longarm's big fist. "You just going to shoot him?"

A nod. "That's my plan."

"No more talking?"

"I can't take another chance like that," Longarm said, pulling a five-cent cheroot out of his coat pocket and then struggling to light it in the wind. He finally got the cigar lit and inhaled deeply a few times. The smoke bit away the last of the heavy sleep lingering on his mind. Its sharp bite allowed him to really focus on what he had to do next.

"Wish me luck," he said, a moment before grabbing the coach door and tearing it open.

He had given the drunk just enough time to crow about running off a United States marshal and to believe that he wasn't in any danger. Just enough time to drop his gun and start browbeating his wife and the other terrified passengers as he tipped the bottle back to his lips.

"Drop the gun!" Longarm shouted, raising his pistol. "Do it right now!"

The man was caught by surprise and his reaction time was shot. He gaped, then cursed as the bottle spilled from his hand and whiskey leaked out of his wide open mouth. Then he lifted his gun to fire.

Longarm shot him in the chest, then again in the throat. Blood gushed from his neck and spurted over the man's wife and son. The drunk twitched, his trigger finger sending an errant bullet into a seat cushion inches from a passenger's head.

Longarm wasn't going to let that happen again so he took careful aim and drilled the drunk right between his hate-filled, bloodshot eyes.

The man fell, dead before he landed atop his family.

"It's going to be all right now," Longarm said to the woman as he shoved her husband aside. "You and the boy are going to be all right."

The woman was in shock and covered with her husband's blood. She began to slap at the blood as if she could make it go away. The other passengers were shouting, some were weeping, others cursing or yelling thanks to their merciful God.

Longarm motioned Albert and another attendant forward. He tried to talk to the woman, but she was numb with shock and totally unresponsive.

"Albert, get her and the boy cleaned up. I'll drag the body out on the platform and fix it to something so it won't fall off the train. And get these other passengers quieted down."

"We'll do it," the conductor promised. "You just shot him deader'n a hat rack. Now what are you going to do?"

"I'm going back to my coach and continue my nap," Longarm told the conductor as he collared the dead man and prepared to drag him out on the platform so that he didn't bleed any more on the carpet.

"You could sleep after what you just did?" Albert asked, looking aghast.

"Yeah," Longarm told him. "I could sleep. There's nothing more for me to do now. You take care of these folks. I'd give them free whiskey from the parlor car, if they wanted. And clean up the blood. There's not much else any of us can do."

Albert nodded and held the door open as Longarm dragged his victim outside and tied him down with his belt and necktie. "Marshal, I don't know how you can sleep after what you just did. I just don't know."

Longarm stood and placed his big hand on the conductor's thin shoulder. "The way I see it, Albert, I didn't really kill that man. I tried to give him a way out, but he refused me. As far as I'm concerned, he is the cause of his own death. He chose to die and I just made sure that he did it without taking me or someone else with him."

"I . . . I understand."

Longarm doubted that Albert did understand. Even though the West was wild and often cruel, most folks never saw brutal killings because they strove to live right with decency. And, on the rare occasions when death did come up and howl in their faces, they found it very hard to accept. But Longarm knew that death could come at any time. He also had learned that some people didn't want to live anymore. The better ones took their own lives and tried not to spread any more havoc or heartache than necessary. But the bad ones . . . those corrupted by fear or hatred . . . wanted good and innocent people to accompany them to the grave.

The drunk, at bottom, had been terminally corrupted and Longarm knew that you either killed them quick . . . or they killed you.

It was just that simple, really.

Chapter 14

"Wake up," the conductor said, gently shaking Longarm as the train pulled into Cheyenne just as the sun was going down. "Will you be connecting up and taking the train west?"

"I'm not sure," Longarm replied with a yawn. "I'm after a couple and they could have gone either east or west. I'm hoping that I can make that determination this evening."

"I want to thank you for what you did for us," Albert told him. "That was as bad a situation as I've ever been in during all my years working on this line. You know, a lot of men tend to drink too much. It's as if once they're out of a town and on their way to another place, they kind of let loose. But this fella, he was purely no good."

"You got that right. How are his widow and son?"

"They're doing better. I talked to the woman and she seemed more relieved than sad. And I understand they have a house paid for in Laramie plus some money in the bank, so she'll do all right."

"She's banged up bad right now but I expect she's normally quite a good-looking woman. If she isn't ruined entirely on men, she'll have a lot of suitors knocking at her door."

"I expect that's true. She asked to see you. Her name is Mrs. Carole Tanner. I think she wants to tell you how grateful she is for saving her and her son from being hurt. Mrs. Tanner confessed to me that her husband had threatened to kill her if she ever left him."

"When you see her, tell her no thanks is necessary." Longarm shifted his weight uncomfortably; he did not want to be thanked for doing something that needed to be done. "Say, Albert, how are the other passengers in first class? That wasn't a pretty scene with all that blood and bullets flying in such close quarters."

"Some of them are doing a lot better than others. They're all pretty upset, as you would expect. But they understand that what happened was unavoidable."

"When Mrs. Tanner gets to Cheyenne," Longarm said, "she needs to visit a doctor."

"We'll make sure she does and the railroad will foot the bill," the conductor assured him. "And we've got to make arrangements for Mr. Tanner to be buried in Laramie. I'm sure we'll pay for that, too. But, Marshal, I can't tell you how hard it was for me not to push that bastard's body off the train and let the vultures and coyotes feast on his foul carcass."

"I understand. It's what the man deserves." Longarm grabbed his bag of extra clothing. "Now Albert, you won't forget your promise to give me first class on the way back to Denver?"

"Not a chance. You're a hero in the eyes of all of us, Marshal Long. If you hadn't killed that crazy bastard, some of us would be dead."

"I'll see you later," Longarm told the conductor as he headed down the aisle.

"Saints protect you, Marshal."

As he exited the train, passengers that had already disembarked from the first-class coach broke out in applause. Longarm was embarrassed and kept walking but a woman hurried over. She grabbed his hand and pumped it up and down saying, "Thank you for saving us, Marshal. And I know that God will forgive you for taking another man's life."

"Glad to hear it," Longarm told her.

"Yes, thank you," a man added, his voice choked with emotion. "We'll never forget what you did today. You're the bravest man I've ever known. You deserve a medal or something. I'd like to write your superior and recommend some kind of award."

"I appreciate the thought but I was just doin' my job," he said a moment before hurrying off toward the combination telegraph office and railroad ticket booth.

Longarm knew that the westbound left around six o'clock the next morning and that it was better to buy his ticket this evening. He also hoped he could find out from the ticket master if Lilly Claire and Edward had taken the westbound on their way to Salt Lake City.

"Excuse me," he said, leaning toward a man who was concentrating on counting money. "I need some information."

"Our westbound leaves at six-o-five tomorrow morning. Eastbound leaves at ten-thirty," the man clipped without even bothering to look up. "Tell me your destination and I'll tell you the fare."

"I don't know my destination yet," Longarm said, annoyed at the man for not giving him his full attention.

"You don't know your destination?" The man still did not look up from his counting.

"No."

117

"Then I can't possibly help you, sir. Please step aside so that someone else can be served."

Longarm had just killed a man and he was in no mood to be brushed aside or treated with disrespect. He reached over the counter and grabbed the ticket master by the front of his shirt. "Look you, put the damned money down and listen to me or I'll bust your beak!"

Now he had the man's full and undivided attention. "Sir, there's no need to be violent!"

"I'm a violent man when I'm ignored." Longarm's voice hardened. "I'm also a deputy United States marshal out of Denver on the trail of possible murderers."

"Yes, sir!"

Longarm released the man and took a deep breath so that he could speak without anger. He told the ticket master in as few words as possible his situation and described Lilly and Edward. He ended by saying, "They would have come through here yesterday . . . or possibly even the day before. They were a very handsome young couple and they'd have had to buy tickets. What I need to know is where they were going."

The man nodded rapidly. "I remember them very well. I even remember where they were headed."

"And?"

"They bought one-way tickets to Salt Lake City."

Longarm relaxed. "That's what I was hoping to hear."

"Good," the ticket master said. "Anything else?"

"Yes. Tell me your impression of the lady."

"Impression? I don't understand."

"Did she seem nervous or frightened?"

"No."

"Did she pay for the tickets or did the man?"

"*She* paid. I remember because it is rather unusual for the wife to pay rather than the husband."

"Did she say he was her husband?"

The ticket master chewed his lower lip. "No, but it seemed quite obvious that they were husband and wife."

"Why obvious?"

"Because he never let her go. They struck me as being newlyweds. Honeymooners."

"Not hardly," Longarm said. "Give me a round-trip ticket to Salt Lake City, Utah."

"Yes, sir. Are you of the Mormon faith?"

"That'll be the day. How much?"

The ticket master didn't have to consult his fare schedule. "Forty-two dollars and fifty-five cents for coach round-trip."

"And first class?"

"Eighty dollars with a private sleeping compartment and meals included."

Longarm hated to fork over such a large part of his travel money, but after what he'd gone through on his way down from Denver, he wanted privacy that included a little luxury. He deserved that much, and if Billy objected later, so what?

"First class," he said, paying the fare.

"My, but Denver lawmen must be a lot better paid than I thought," the ticket master said cryptically. "Must be nice to charge it all to the taxpayers."

Longarm had an urge to slap the smirk off the man's face, but he'd had enough trouble for one day. So he collected his ticket and left without another word.

When he got into town, Longarm went straight to the Cattleman's Hotel where he was in the habit of staying while waiting for a train connection. The Cattleman's had a nice saloon and restaurant and Longarm was well known and respected by the hotel's friendly and efficient staff.

"Good evening, Marshal Long!" the hotel desk clerk said with a grin. He was in his mid-twenties, good-looking and unfailingly cheerful. "I hear you permanently cooled some crazy on the train coming up from Denver."

"Josh, I had to kill him, if that's what you mean."

"That's exactly what I mean," the young man said, his eyes filled with admiration. "Cooled him. Drilled him. Drained his brain. Whatever. It's all the same thing. Anyway, we all heard about it and the manager says that your room and meals are on the house. And I've reserved one of our finest suites."

"For a fact?"

"Sure!" Joshua rubbed his hands briskly together. "Marshal, you're a big celebrity in Cheyenne. If you go into the saloon, there will be folks there just begging to buy you drinks. I'd buy you one myself if I wasn't stuck at this desk until midnight."

"What's the big deal?"

"Roscoe Tanner was thoroughly disliked in Cheyenne. He was a cattle buyer. A prize jerk. And everyone knew he had a nice family but that didn't stop him from getting drunk then going over to the whorehouses beyond the tracks. One night, he got so drunk he brought one of them two-dollar whores right into this hotel. Can you imagine the gall?"

"I'm sure it wasn't appreciated."

"You can say that again. Tanner attempted to escort the whore through the lobby and up to his room. I put a stop to that in a big hurry, but he raised hell. I wanted to punch his face in, but I didn't even though he tried to put his knee into my balls. But I knocked him down and sat on his chest until he gave up the struggle."

"Then what happened?"

"I was afraid that my action had cost me my job, but it

120

didn't. Our hotel manager took my side and told Mr. Tanner in no uncertain terms that he was never to come back into the Cattleman's Hotel. He said that we didn't need Tanner's business."

"I'm glad you didn't lose your job," Longarm said. "And the management was right to ban him from this place because some of the most important people in Wyoming stay here regularly."

"That's right and they don't expect to see drunks and whores being paraded around," Josh said, nodding vigorously. "Why, that Tanner fella would get drunk and start fights in our saloon. We were all glad when the management finally banned him from this hotel."

"Well," Longarm said, "I hope his young wife finds a good man to take his place."

"Oh, she will! Don't worry about that, Marshal. Mrs. Carole Tanner is one of the best-looking women in town and her son is a fine boy." Josh sighed. "I already overheard a few gentlemen say that they'll be calling on her after a proper period of grieving. But I wouldn't wait. Why should she grieve? If you ask me, Carole Tanner ought to be celebrating with champagne."

"I expect that is true enough. The woman took a vicious beating before I cooled her husband down permanently. She's probably on her way to the doctor right now."

The desk clerk's face darkened with rage. "If you hadn't shot him, someone else would have . . . and it probably would have been me."

Longarm cocked an eyebrow. "Sounds like you've got a crush on Mrs. Tanner."

Josh blushed. "I'm just a desk clerk. I'm the head desk clerk, but that's nothing special. They're saying I'll manage this place someday but you know praise won't put a roof over a family's head or food on the table."

"How old are you, Josh?"

"Twenty-one."

"You're going to be a success no matter where you go," Longarm said. "And what would you have to lose by buying Mrs. Tanner some flowers or sending her a card expressing your condolences?"

"Aw," he said with a shrug of his wide shoulders. "Miss Tanner probably wouldn't even know who I was."

"Then take them over to her house tomorrow and show her who you are," Longarm urged. "Why wait for some other man to step in and fill the void in her and her son's life."

"The other gentlemen are wealthy, that's why," Josh said. "They're cattle ranchers and business owners. I've got nothing."

"Never underestimate yourself, Josh. Because, in my experience, that's the cause of most men's failure. Be bold and optimistic. Above all, take pride in yourself and know you're about as good as the next man and better than most."

The young man grinned. "Marshal, do you *really* mean that?"

"I sure do. But I have a warning for you about Mrs. Tanner."

"Yes, sir?"

"She'll be bad down on men. After all, her husband was a cheat and an all-around snake. What that means is that she very likely won't trust any man for quite some time. And the one that she finally does trust will have to win her heart and be very patient and gentle."

Josh nodded. "I am patient and gentle. And I do worship the ground that woman walks upon. But . . ."

"But nothing," Longarm interrupted. "Life is a prize, but you have to win it by persistence and hard work. Nothing comes for free. Not the love of a special woman or financial success. Not that I've had much financial success. But that's because it was never my priority. I could make big money if I really put my mind to it, and so could you."

Josh stood taller. "By jingo, you're getting me fired up! I'm going to take the woman flowers first thing tomorrow morning and offer to help her in any way I can."

"And," Longarm said, "if she refuses your help . . . because you are a stranger . . . don't lose heart. Keep at it and you'll eventually win her over while all those other suitors are just standing around waiting for the mourning period to pass."

"I'll do just that, Marshal!"

"I'll be watching to make sure that you do," Longarm told the young desk clerk. "And now, if you don't mind, I think I'll take to my room."

"But don't you want to go into the saloon and get those free drinks everyone is itchin' to buy you?"

"I'm going to pass on that," he said. "I've got an early departure tomorrow and I want to be rested when I leave Cheyenne."

"Where you headed this time?"

"Salt Lake City."

"On the trail of killers or bank robbers?"

"I'm not sure. Murderers, perhaps."

Josh sighed. "You sure lead an exciting life, Marshal. There are times when I think I'd like to be just like you."

"But, if you did, you wouldn't be around to win the heart of the widow Tanner, now would you?"

"No, sir, I guess not."

"Then stick to your plan and stay right here in Cheyenne where you can win the bigger prize. And you do like children, don't you?"

"Love 'em. Want to have at least a dozen."

"Well, I'm anything but an authority on these things, but if I were you, I'd also take a toy or two whenever I called on Miss Tanner. Mothers put a lot of stock in a man who would love their children."

"I'll do 'er! I'll buy the little fella a real fine fishin' pole. Do you think he's old enough for that?"

Longarm had to laugh as he took his room key and headed upstairs for a good night's sleep.

Chapter 15

Longarm was on the westbound train for Utah bright and early the next morning. He'd gotten a full eight hours of sleep and felt better than he had in a week. The conductor told him that it was 435 miles between Cheyenne and Salt Lake City and most of it was flat sage and rather ugly. But this first part of the journey was scenic. Longarm watched with interest as the train struggled over the beautiful Laramie Mountains. Along the way he saw lots of deer, elk and even a number of huge beaver ponds. The air was high and cool with lots of aspen and pine and some of the higher peaks were still mantled with glistening snow, even this late in the summer.

The train finally crossed the rugged mountains and then eased down their western slope into Laramie to take on coal and water. Laramie was one of Longarm's favorite towns with its wide streets lined with shade-giving cottonwoods, well manicured yards and friendly citizens. While the train was taking on coal and water Longarm had a bite to eat and then shopped, buying ammunition and a new folding pocketknife from a blacksmith who was renowned for the quality of his blades.

He still had over a hundred dollars and it felt great to be riding in first-class coach with his own sleeping compartment.

He asked around, and sure enough, quite a few people remembered seeing an attractive couple that fit the description of Lilly and Edward. And one of the witnesses remembered that Edward had kept a close watch on the beautiful but withdrawn blond woman at his side as they'd wandered through the shopping district.

"I remember he clung to her like a bumblebee to a sweet honey pot," the woman said. "That tall man never let her out of his sight for a minute. It was almost as if he was afraid that she might run off and leave him."

"Thanks," Longarm said, wondering again what was going on between the pair. He didn't know if Edward was a murderer or not but he sure meant to find out and put to rest the identity of the woman buried under a tombstone marked Lilly Claire.

He boarded the train, found his private compartment and relaxed as the flat and unspectacular country rolled past. Rawlins was a rough railroad town that rivaled Rock Springs in its struggle to survive and escape obscurity. Both towns had honest and competent local marshals but Longarm knew they were dangerous places where railroad workers, cowboys and Indians brawled every night in a dozen rough and ready saloons. The only thing that seemed to be growing in either of the railroad towns were their cemeteries. Out in this flat, largely treeless sage land, the wind blew hard and constant. It was a tough place to survive, much less prosper.

After Rock Springs there was historic Fort Bridger now abandoned except for a stable, saloon and trading post; after that the land began to rise and green up leaving the gray sage. By the second day out of Cheyenne they were climbing the rugged and still mostly untamed Wasatch Range.

"We'll be in Salt Lake City by evening," the conductor said that afternoon. "I see from your ticket that you will be leaving us there."

"That's right."

"Enjoy your stay in Salt Lake," the man told him without much enthusiasm.

Longarm doubted that he would enjoy his stay in Brigham Young's stronghold. It wasn't that he had anything against members of the Church of the Latter Day Saints, it was just that he didn't share anything in common. Being a drinker and a cigar smoker, he stood out on the streets in that squeaky clean and well-planned city. And he had never had much cooperation from the Mormon authorities. They were an independent bunch, many of them polygamists and not wanting anything to do with the United States and especially its distrusted and always intruding federal officers.

Longarm got off the train and found a hotel downtown. He didn't quite know where to start so he spent the first day just walking around, asking people on the street if they had seen a couple that fit the description of Lilly and Edward.

But that approach got him nothing so he reluctantly visited the marshal's office and found that he was about as welcome there as a polecat at a picnic.

"We'll keep an eye out for them," the marshal told him knowing full well he wouldn't. "And where can you be reached on the off chance that we do see the young couple that you've just described?"

"I'll be around until I pick up their trail. I guess I'll start asking at all the hotels next."

"Maybe you should have one of my men as your escort."

"That won't be necessary."

"Yes, it will."

Longarm could see that, in Salt Lake City, you either did things their way or you didn't get them done. "Fine."

He was assigned an officer named Caleb Bass. Bass was a nice enough man in his forties. He was solid, wore a full beard but no mustache and never smiled. Caleb Bass was all business especially when he tried to convince Longarm of the wisdom and truth of the Book of Mormon. Because of Longarm's negative reaction to the work, they had an immediate falling out. After that, Bass was worse than having no company at all. He became uncooperative and downright surly.

"Thanks for your time, Officer," Longarm said at the end of a long, fruitless day when they had finally visited all the hotels and gotten nowhere in their search. "I won't be needing you tomorrow."

"What are you going to do next?" the Salt Lake City lawman demanded. Before Longarm could think of an answer, Bass continued. "We don't much appreciate any outsiders, especially a federal officer skulking around asking personal questions. It makes people nervous and uncomfortable. You ought to be able to understand that, Marshal Long."

"I do."

"Then you need to get back on the train and return to Denver."

"I'd like nothing better than to do that," Longarm told Bass as they stood near the great Mormon Temple. "But the truth is, I can't leave until I pick up this couple's trail."

Bass snorted with derision through his bulbous nose. "You never told my superior what it is these people have done wrong."

Trying to keep the conversation on a civil footing, Longarm replied, "That's because I'm not sure myself."

Bass didn't understand that answer and it showed in his disapproving scowl. "What kind of a lawman are you to come all this way and not even know what crime these people have committed?"

It would have been very easy to explain to Deputy Caleb Bass that Longarm was a highly experienced lawman, one who had tracked criminals all over the West without even once failing to catch his quarry. But Longarm knew Bass wouldn't be impressed and so he held his tongue.

"I'll have to write a report on today's wasted effort," Bass continued. "It would help if you would tell me something more about this couple whose guilt or innocence you can't even decide about."

"Sorry," Longarm told him. He managed a thin smile. "But I'm not saying a thing to you or your boss."

Bass flushed with anger. "We'll be seeing about *that*! I don't know who you think you are coming here and causing us to waste our time. But we won't put up with it, and should we hear even one complaint about you . . ."

The Mormon law officer didn't finish. He just let the threat hang, which made it all the more ominous.

"What?" Longarm said, his anger starting to finally rise to the surface. "Are you going to arrest a federal officer for trying to solve what is possibly a murder? Is that what you are telling me?"

Bass backed down. "That's the first time you said you were after murderers."

"I didn't say that," Longarm growled a moment before turning and leaving the man in the street.

That evening, feeling highly frustrated and at loose ends, Longarm trudged back to the railroad station. He wandered around the depot as if he might find some clue as to the whereabouts of Edward and Lilly, all the while knowing he wouldn't.

"Can I help you?" a friendly voice called.

Longarm turned to see a young man sitting in a buggy wearing the usual Mormon garb but also a fine derby hat. He smiled and added, "I'll take you anywhere in town for one dollar. Or, if you'd rather, I'll just show you the finest sites of our great city and it will cost you just two dollars."

Longarm had nothing else to do so he climbed into the carriage and settled back for the two-dollar excursion. It was a warm evening and he wished he could remove his jacket but Salt Lake City was a rather formal town where most of the elders wore a black suit, white shirt and black tie.

"What would you like to see first?"

"It doesn't matter," Longarm answered. "Actually, I'm hunting for someone new to this town."

"A woman?" the young man said boldly.

"A woman *and* a man. They would have arrived here about two days ago." Longarm went on to describe the fugitives and ended by saying, "They were a pair that would catch your eye. A very striking couple."

"And you say they got off the westbound train?"

"That's right."

"Well," the young man said with a shrug of his shoulders. "I'm here every day when the train arrives. It's where I get most of my best fares. And I can tell you that I stand right on the unloading platform and that no such couple departed. Not today, not yesterday and not all week."

"How can you be so sure?"

"I just am." The young man turned around in his seat and looked back at Longarm. "I watch everyone who gets off the train. Most of the passengers are common people. Train workers. Cowboys. Farmers. You know, just good, hardworking people. But when I see a wealthy couple such as you describe, I hurry to offer my assistance and hope to earn a handsome tip. I carry their baggage and tell them lively or interesting stories about our city."

"And you don't remember such a couple getting off here?"

"Nope. Definitely not."

Longarm was nothing less than stunned. When the young man started to raise his whip and drive them away, he shouted, "Hold up!"

"What's wrong?"

"I need to talk to the ticket agent," he said, jumping out of the carriage. "Here's your two dollars."

The young man looked confused. "But I didn't drive you anywhere."

"No, but what you told me makes everything clear now. And . . ." Longarm was so enthused that he gave the young driver two extra dollars. "And now I see where I was completely wrong. I made a bad assumption and I was fooled. Completely outfoxed."

"Sir?"

"Thank you and good evening!" Longarm called as he raced toward the ticket office.

It was all so very clear now. He should have realized that a worldly and sophisticated pair like Lilly and Edward would *never* have been so careless as to have accidentally left a postmarked envelope in their Denver trash. Of course not! That would have been stupid and neither of them were the least bit stupid. So they must have left the envelope knowing that Longarm or some other officer would find it and jump to the wrong conclusion.

"Damn!" he swore as he bounded up on the railroad de-pot platform and hurried over to the ticket and passenger office.

"Excuse me," he said to a pair of bearded men in their thirties who were working in the office. "But I need some help."

"Whatever we can do, sir."

Now that, Longarm thought, *is the right attitude.*

He showed them his badge and then described his quarry. Longarm ended by saying, "This couple would have arrived several days ago. End of the line. They were supposed to get off the train here, but I'm beginning to think they continued on."

"They sure did," the smallest of the pair said as he adjusted his eyeglasses. "I remember them very well. I'm sure you do, too, George."

"Oh, yes," the other one said, trying to hide a smile in his bushy whiskers. "Without any disrespect, that woman was not someone easily overlooked or forgotten."

"What did they do? Where did they go?" Longarm gushed.

The man with the thick glasses asked, "Are they in serious trouble?"

"I don't know. They might be but perhaps not. I won't know until I find them and ask questions."

"She really was quite a beauty. Of course, she was not of our faith, sadly. But all the same, she was extremely reserved but polite."

"A bit nervous," the other Mormon added. "She didn't look all that well."

"What," Longarm asked, "do you mean?"

"Her color was very pale. As if she never saw the light of day."

"Yes," his friend said, "and she never smiled. Even more remarkable was that it was *she*, not the gentleman with her, who paid for the tickets."

"To where?" Longarm asked, trying to keep from shouting.

"To Reno."

Longarm nodded. "Are you absolutely certain?"

"Of course." The man with the glasses opened a thick ledger and traced his forefinger down its pages until he came to a dated entry. "Yes. Two days ago they arrived and immediately came to this counter and bought first-class tickets for Reno. Paid cash. Thirty-seven dollars each. The gentleman wanted nothing but the best and I had to convince him that all the first-class compartments are identical."

"That's not quite true," the other Mormon said. "We know that some are nicer than others. We gave them the best available and they even gave us each a dollar in tips. We don't often accept them but the man was insistent that we accept."

"Oops!" The one with the glasses covered his mouth with his hand.

"What?" Longarm asked.

"The gentleman asked us not to say to anyone that they had extended their first-class tickets so that they could go on to Reno."

The two young men looked at each other, probably feeling they'd betrayed a trust. But Longarm didn't care.

"I'll take a first class to Reno." He opened his wallet and quickly reconsidered. He hadn't even begun the real work that he'd been sent from Denver to accomplish. "I'd better make that a coach fare."

"Yes, sir. If you do find that couple, please don't tell the gentleman that we told you where he and his wife were bound."

"I promise I won't," Longarm said solemnly.

He counted out his money and said, "When is the west-bound coming through?"

"I'm sorry but it departs here at midnight."

"That's fine."

"We really hate to tell people that but it labors across the great salt flats and its blistering heat out there. That's why they travel it in the middle of the night."

The one with the glasses added, "And because it's so ugly between here and Reno."

"Yes, of course," Longarm said, paying his money and taking his ticket. He consulted his pocket watch and realized that he had almost four hours to get his bags from his hotel and then wait.

And the worst part of it was that he couldn't even find a saloon or a bottle of liquor to help him pass the long hours in the doldrums of Salt Lake City.

Chapter 16

Longarm was on his way again, only this time to Reno, Nevada, a town that he had always liked. He boarded the train at midnight and slept right through the Great Salt Lake Basin. In the morning, they made a stop in dusty Elko for fuel and water while loading several boxcars with thin cattle pulled off a range that offered little nourishment. Then, they followed the Truckee River across northeastern Nevada crossing vast oceans of sagebrush, pinion pine and juniper.

There wasn't much to see in that huge, open country. Several times, Longarm saw cattle being herded by cowboys and once a flock of sheep tended to by a band of ragged Paiute Indians.

Battle Mountain and then on to Winnemucca named after Sarah Winnemucca, a famous Indian maiden. These were dusty railroad towns with a few saloons and business that catered mostly to the big ranches and their lonesome buckaroos. Other than that, there was very little to see so Longarm did a lot of napping that day as the train traced the line of the fading Humboldt River until even that petered out and disappeared in the sand and blazing basin heat.

"Reno is comin' up in about ten minutes," the porter announced. "Be good to get home and see the family again."

The man was in his fifties, short and slight but he was cheerful and ready to please even the half dozen or so coach passengers. Longarm had been stretched out on a wooden bench and now he sat up and stretched. "And how big a family do you have?"

"Wife and five children," the man replied. "Three boys and two girls. Couldn't ask for better'n that."

"You want to have any more?"

The porter smiled. "I'm always ready, willin' and plenty eager to give it a try, but the missus, she has other ideas. She says five kids are more than enough. And I guess they are since I'm gone half the time on this train. My usual run takes me all the way to Saint Louis and back. I enjoy it but miss my family. Got a chance to become a conductor in the next few years and that will mean a big raise. Good jobs out here are hard to come by and I'm not about to quit this one . . . although sometimes the missus wishes I would."

"I understand."

The porter looked at him. "Word is that you're on the trail of a pair of killers, Marshal. A man *and* a woman."

"Who told you that?"

"There are no secrets on a train. Besides, why would a man like you be going out over country like this unless it was a manhunt?"

"Well," Longarm said, seeing no point in trying to hide the fact, "I am after a pair. You ever heard of Miss Lilly Claire?"

"Sure. She's a rich and famous singer and dancer.

136

She's performed a lot on the Comstock Lode. I understand she's quite a sensation."

"Maybe you heard that she died in Denver."

"No," the man answered, his smile dying, "I did not hear that."

"Anyway, the whole case is pretty confusing," Longarm said. "I'm going to tie up some loose ends."

"I've seen Miss Claire travel on this train more than once," the man said. "She went from city to city for her big engagements. I'm real sorry to hear she died."

Longarm figured he'd said enough so he lit a cigar and patiently waited as the train rolled into Reno. The town marshal's name was Bill Tate and he was a longtime friend. Tate had been a cowboy before he'd gotten tired of riding the dusty Nevada deserts chasing starving animals and trying not to get scalped by the Paiutes who still hated and resented the white men who had intruded upon their lands. Tate was in his forties now but he was still tough and lean. He'd learned the hard way how to take care of the town even though the lessons he'd learned had often nearly cost him his life.

When Longarm disembarked and headed up Virginia Street toward the Truckee River and the old Maple Hotel, he made a stop at Bill Tate's office where he found the lawman reading catalogues.

"Hello, Bill," he said. "How's the easy life?"

The cowboy turned lawman grinned. Tate was a tall, thin man who didn't let much of anything disturb him. He had a chubby wife and a few kids as well as a little frame house. Tate wasn't a man who asked a lot of life, but he wasn't a man you wanted to push around, either. He had invested his hard-earned money in good weapons and he'd not stinted on the ammunition it took to learn how to shoot them straight and fast. Longarm knew for a fact that Tate had shot down no less than five men and that his reputation as a crack shot now discouraged troublemakers from putting Reno's town marshal to the test.

"Well I do declare, it's deputy United States Marshal Custis Long! What in the devil brings you clear out to my fair city by the Sierras?"

"It's a strange case, Bill. Got some coffee?"

"I'll make a fresh pot. In the meantime, you can start your story."

Longarm told the town marshal all about Lilly Claire and her alleged brother, Edward. Tate already knew most of that, but when the coffee was brewed and poured, Tate was astonished to learn the rest of the Denver story.

"You mean she hired you to protect her from some unknown assassin and then she just up and disappeared?"

"That's pretty much the short of it," Longarm said.

"Well she must have been foolin' you all along."

"I saw the threatening letters, Bill. And I'm sure that Lilly felt her life was in great danger. Then, when she was supposedly killed and I was nearly shot to death in that city park ambush, I knew that something was very wrong. I thought I'd failed Miss Claire until I discovered it wasn't her that was really buried in the city cemetery."

"Someone switched the bodies?"

"Yep."

"But why would anyone, especially Miss Claire, do such a bizarre thing?"

"I have no idea," Longarm replied. "It's the damnedest mystery I've had to solve in my entire law career. All I can think of is that this Edward fella, who was supposed to be Lilly's brother, is behind all the trouble. He must want something that Lilly has . . . only he has to keep her alive and get her back here to collect it."

"Life insurance?"

138

Longarm shrugged. "That's sure one possibility I've considered. Does Miss Claire live in Reno?"

"No. She spends more of her time up in Virginia City where I understand Comstock Lode miners worship the ground on which she walks. But she also spends her winters in San Francisco."

"I need to find her fast. Something is very wrong and I'm afraid her life is in great danger."

"I'll do whatever I can to help. However, I doubt that she's in Reno. She usually just passes through town, although I think she does some banking and business here."

"Do you know which bank?"

Bill thought about that for several moments. "I believe I've seen her coming and going from the Bank of Nevada. It's right up the street."

"How about introducing me to the bank manager?" Longarm asked. "I'll need to get a look at her account and bankers can be pretty standoffish about doing that, even for an officer of the law."

"His name is Arnold Parks. He and I get along real well so I think he'll help us out," Bill said, downing his coffee and then reaching for his hat. "Let's go on over and see what the man has to say."

"If Miss Claire still has money in his bank, he ought to be able to tell us that much, at least. And, if she doesn't, then I'll need to find out when she cleaned out her account."

"I understand," Bill said.

When they met Mr. Parks, he listened carefully, but a frown began to grow on his face. "I can't open someone's account."

"It's a federal matter, Mr. Parks. It could have serious

repercussions on your bank if you don't cooperate." Longarm wanted and needed this man's full cooperation so he added, "And I don't need to know the exact balance in Miss Claire's personal account."

Parks was obviously a worrier. He led them back to his office at the rear of the bank and sat down at his desk. He picked up a pencil, twirled it around absently in his hand for a moment as he considered this request, then laid the pencil down and leaned forward so that both elbows rested on the desk.

"All right," he said, "I'll go ask one of my tellers to look up Miss Claire's account."

"Mainly, I need to know if she withdrew all or most of her money in the last day or two," Longarm said. "Also, if the account is in her name only."

Parks went off and was gone for only a few minutes. When he reappeared, he was studying a piece of paper and didn't look a bit pleased. "This is very upsetting."

"What is?" both Longarm and Bill Tate asked simultaneously.

"Miss Claire closed her account two days ago. She withdrew nearly eight thousand dollars."

"In cash?"

"Yes. And that is *very* unwise." He shook his bald head and ran a finger under his black tie. "We could have and should have issued Miss Claire a cashier's check. For her own safety we almost never hand out that large a sum of money. I should have been consulted and I'm extremely upset that my signature wasn't requested for transaction approval."

Longarm wasn't any more pleased than the bank manager. "I'd like you to bring the person who authorized this withdrawal into your office. I have some questions that need to be asked."

"Yes. That would be a very good idea. His name is Mr. Mike Howell. He's my assistant. This is very, very troubling."

A few minutes later, Mr. Howell appeared and was ordered to take a chair.

"What's this about, Mr. Parks?" the younger man asked, looking at Longarm and the town marshal with great concern. "Is something wrong?"

"There certainly is," Carter said, displaying a paper. "Why wasn't I consulted about this withdrawal by Miss Claire? At the very least, I should have signed off on the transaction."

"You were at lunch, sir. The lady was in a great hurry and quite demanding that her account be closed and that she be given cash. I told her that we would prefer to give her a cashier's check but she insisted that it be cash." Howell shrugged. "And since she is well known and highly regarded, I didn't think that you would disagree with my decision."

Longarm stepped forward. "Was the account in her name only?"

"Yes. Who are you?"

Longarm showed the man his badge. "How would you describe Miss Claire's physical appearance?"

"She was radiant as always and appeared to me to be in perfect health." Howell looked to his boss. "Mr. Parks, I'm confused and I wish to know what these questions are all about."

The banker was still peeved at his assistant. "The reasons behind these questions are not your concern. And as for your giving the woman cash without my approval, we'll discuss that mistake later."

Howell sighed. "Yes, sir."

The assistant manager was starting to look ill and Longarm almost felt sorry for the man. Under the same circumstances, he'd also have given Miss Claire her cash. After all, it was her money. "Mr. Howell, I know that Miss Claire can be very persuasive, and under the circumstances, I'm sure that you did what you thought best both for her and for the Bank of Nevada."

"I always try to do what I think is best," he said, thoroughly deflated.

"I'm sure you do," Longarm told the man. "Now, I need to know the color of her hair when Miss Claire arrived to close out her bank account."

Howell's confusion was evident to everyone in the office, but he stammered, "Why, the same as it's always been. Lustrous black." Confusion was turning to anger. "Marshal, would you like to also know the color of her eyes?"

Longarm shook his head. He knew the color of Lilly's eyes as well as the shape of her luscious body.

"She's reverted back to her true self," he said to his friend, Marshal Tate. "Miss Claire has gotten rid of the blond wig she was wearing as a disguise when she fled Denver."

"One last question," Longarm said, turning back to the bankers. "Was Miss Claire alone or with her brother, Edward?"

"She was escorted into the foyer of the bank by a man that I've never seen before," the assistant bank manager said.

Longarm leaned forward. "Describe him."

Howell composed himself for a moment, obviously trying to remember every detail. "I didn't pay him much attention and he stood near the front door while I conducted my transaction with the lady. But I remember he was rather tall, though not as tall as yourself, Marshal."

"About six feet tall?"

"Yes," Howell said, "that would be about right. The gentleman removed his hat and he had rather long brown hair. My impression was that he was an artist, or a thespian and I thought him distinguished-looking."

"How was he dressed?"

"Very much like yourself. His clothes were well tailored and clean. He wore a tie and his shoes were polished."

The banker, Mr. Parks, was impressed. "Mike, your powers of observation are rather remarkable."

"Thank you, sir." Howell stood up straighter. "I always watch the people who enter our bank very closely. One can never be too careful."

"Quite right," Parks agreed.

Longarm was thinking hard and suddenly remembered that Edward had combed his hair parted down the *left* side and wore no facial hair. "How did this man part his hair?"

Howell frowned. "I am quite sure he parted his hair down the middle."

"Was the man clean-shaven or did he have a mustache or beard?"

"He had both a mustache and beard," Howell said without hesitation. "The mustache was very much like yours and he had a small goatee rather than a full beard."

"You are being very helpful," Longarm said to the assistant banker. "Would you recognize this man if you saw him again?"

"Of course."

"Was he armed?"

"He wasn't wearing a pistol on a gun belt, if that's what you mean. But he gave the impression that he would carry a hideout gun."

"What gave you that impression?"

Howell pursed his lips in thought. "I can't say exactly. But my feeling was that he was a man who would never allow himself to be at a disadvantage in a difficult situation. He looked . . . well, the gentleman had a look that said he could be dangerous, if pushed. He looked like someone who had commanded men in the Civil War. He had that kind of bearing."

The town marshal had a question. "Did he have any scars or notable physical marks that would help us recognize him."

"As a matter of fact, he did."

"And that would be?"

Howell smiled like a schoolroom boy who had answered an especially difficult question for his proud teacher. "The gentleman that escorted Miss Claire into our bank had one *very* noticeable feature."

Longarm waited and when Howell paused for effect, Longarm snapped, "Spit it out, sir."

"Very well," Howell said, "the gentleman was missing his lower left arm."

"Are you sure?" Marshal Tate asked.

"Oh, yes. I'm as sure as I live and breathe. I remember that the sleeve was long, not pinned up. And instead of a human hand, he wore a polished wooden club shaped rather like a hand."

"Are you certain?" Longarm asked, wondering if he had heard correctly.

"Yes. When the device rested at his side, it was the exact same length as his right hand and not very noticeable."

"How unusual," Longarm mused.

"And the gentleman had a cane in his right . . . his real hand. A very fine cane with a silver handle. He tapped the cane repeatedly on the lobby floor as he waited. I could hear it and it made me think the gentleman was quite impatient. It also seemed to upset Miss Claire, and she looked back at the one-armed gentleman several times as if to assure him that everything was going well and she would soon have her money."

"My!" the bank manager said, obviously impressed. "You really amaze me, Mr. Howell."

"My secret hobby has always been watching interesting people. I believe it is an asset in this profession. At least I hope it is, sir."

"Why it most certainly is," the banker said, clearly no longer upset with his assistant. "Marshal, despite Mike's breach of judgment regarding the large cash disbursal, he has done exceedingly well, don't you think?"

Both Longarm and Marshal Tate nodded in agreement.

Longarm was ready to leave. He had found out what he had to know. Now, all he needed to do was to find Miss Claire before it was too late, because he had a feeling she was about to die.

Chapter 17

Longarm spent the rest of that day looking around Reno for Miss Claire, Edward and whoever the third man was who had accompanied Lilly into the bank. Marshal Tate was a real help in this search because he knew everyone in his town.

At the end of the day, the town marshal said, "She's not here, Custis. And neither are the other two men you're searching for."

"Then you think she might be up in Virginia City?"

"That's where I'd go next if I were you," the marshal replied. "I'd go with you but my deputy got hurt in a saloon fight he was trying to break up so I don't have any backup."

"When does the next stage leave for the Comstock Lode?"

"Tomorrow morning at nine o'clock. You'll arrive in Virginia City around noon."

"Then I'll be on it," he said. "I'd better get a room at the Maple Hotel."

Tate said, "If you could wait a few days until my deputy

is feeling better, I'd go up there with you. Could be some big trouble in store."

"I appreciate the offer," Longarm said, "but I've come this far and I don't want to take the chance of missing Lilly again. Besides that, I think her life is in great danger."

"I sure hope that's not the case," Tate said. "And I wish you luck."

Longarm got a room and then went into the hotel's small but richly decorated saloon. It was called the Roundup Room and the walls were decorated with the heads of cattle with enormous horn spreads. There were also pictures of some of Nevada's most prominent local buckaroos and cattlemen. The floor was covered with clean sawdust and Longarm appreciated the long bar that was so highly polished it glistened under the hanging chandeliers. Longarm patronized the Roundup Room because the customers were congenial and interesting; also the saloon's liquor was premium grade.

"Why bless my soul if it isn't Marshal Custis Long!" a voice called.

Longarm was leaning against the bar with an excellent Kentucky whiskey in his fist as he turned to see a woman whose face and figure he remembered but whose name he had forgotten.

She was a striking woman in her mid-thirties, slender with reddish-blond hair. She wore a red dress that plunged at the neckline and red silk stockings. Suddenly, he recalled that she was a part owner of this hotel and married to a gambling man that everyone called "Shake."

"You've forgotten my name, haven't you, bad boy?" she asked as she came up close and gave him a strong hug and then a kiss on the lips. "I ought to be crushed."

"Your name is Rosie," he said, the beautiful woman's

name coming to him suddenly. "Rosie Red O'Brien and you're still easily the most beautiful woman in Reno. Probably all of Nevada."

"Ah, all is forgiven! And you're still the handsomest marshal to ever walk into this saloon. And so what brings you to Reno?"

Longarm knew that others were listening and he didn't want his purpose to be widely known. "Oh, you know, Rosie, the usual business."

She waited and when he said no more, she nodded with understanding. "And it's bound to be bloody business, I'm sure. Why don't you ever come to Reno just for fun? You and I could light up this town together."

"You light it up all by yourself, Rosie. So how is your old boyfriend Shake?"

At the mention of his name, Rosie scoffed. "Well, he finally got what he deserved and that was a bullet in the gizzard. Shake is six feet under and I'm long past the mourning."

"What happened?" Longarm remembered Shake as being a handsome gambler as fast and smooth with a hideout gun as he was with dealing from the bottom of the deck.

"Shake was shot cheating at cards last January. I'd been telling him for weeks that he was losing his touch. When I met him last summer he could deal from the bottom of the deck faster than the blink of the human eye. But he began drinking too much and his fingertips lost that precious touch. Then, one day another gambler called him a cheat. When the gunsmoke settled, my Shake was lying on the floor shaking hands with the devil. He died in my arms begging my forgiveness for all the bad things he said and did to me while we were together."

"I'm sorry to hear that," Longarm said. "I didn't know Shake, but he always seemed to be a real charmer."

"Oh, he was that all right," Rosie answered. "When Shake was good, he was *very* good, but when he was bad he made my life a living hell. He spent more money than I could make and I'd have had to sell out my interest in this hotel if he'd lived much longer."

"Is that so?"

Rosie ordered a special whiskey that she kept behind the bar and her eyes were misty. "Not only could my Shake spend money faster than any man I ever met, but he was a fool for betting on horse races. He'd buy horses and race them. Almost always his horses would lose a bundle and then he'd be up to his neck in debt with nowhere to go but to me for a loan. And you know what really frosted the cake?"

"Nope."

"One of his longtime mistresses was this town's most respected schoolteacher!"

"I'll be darned."

Rosie dabbed the tears from her eyes. "I know it's wrong to speak of the dead, but Shake lived to corrupt a town's most respectable women. Besides the schoolmarm, he also bedded the wife of the most prominent preacher in Reno. Ruined the poor man of the cloth and broke his heart."

"Some men are just bad to the core, Rosie."

"That was Shake, all right." Rosie downed her whiskey and received an immediate refill. "The minister's wife became hysterical and cut her wrists, but she wasn't really serious about it and didn't die. She and her preacher husband left town before she was tarred and feathered by the congregation. As for the schoolteacher, she'll never teach the young ones in Nevada again. She was lucky to get out of Reno with her life. I'm not one to judge others and lord knows I'm far from being a moral woman, but someone who teaches children ought to be held to a higher standard, don't you agree?"

"I do," Longarm said as Rosie sniffed and dabbed tears from her eyes, telling him that she had loved Shake, despite his considerable failings.

Rosie squared her shoulders and laughed. "To hell with Shake! This town . . . in fact, this entire country is far better off without that two-timing rat."

"I agree."

Rosie hugged him again. "Marshal, I'd like to show you something that you might find interesting."

"All right."

"Follow me," Rosie said.

Longarm followed the woman out the door and up some back stairs to an upstairs room. Rosie unlocked the door and said, "Come on in."

Her room was completely decorated in red. Red lace curtains, red bedspread and red velvet upholstery. Longarm was quite impressed. "Rosie," he asked, "how come you are so in love with the color red?"

She poured them both some very expensive brandy from France and considered the question a moment before answering. "I guess it's because the color red makes me feel happy and it brings me luck."

She held the French brandy up to a lamp. "What color is it, Custis?"

He squinted. "Why, this brandy definitely has a beautiful amber and reddish cast. Highly unusual."

"That's because it has just a hint of cherry-mint flavoring. Would you like to try some?"

"As long as it isn't too sweet."

Red poured him a drink and Longarm found it better

than expected, although it wasn't something he could drink on a regular basis. "Rosie, what is it that you wanted to show me?"

"This room. Did you know that my father was a Texas Ranger?"

"No."

She found a tintype that showed a very good-looking man holding a rifle and looking all business. "He was a famous Ranger out of Austin. He was also my hero and I've always had a thing for lawmen. I have a thing for our town marshal, Big Bill Tate . . . not that it does me much good because he's devoted to his family and is an honorable man completely unlike Shake."

"Yes," Longarm said, not having a clue as to where this conversation was leading. "Marshal Tate sets a high standard both as a lawman and as a person."

Rosie set her drink down and slipped her hands around Longarm's neck. "*You* don't have a family, do you, Custis?"

"Never been married."

"That's what I thought," Rosie said. "So how about you and me having a little fun? I haven't seen a man nearly as handsome as poor old Shake until you walked through the door. And you're just the one to help me finally put Shake to rest."

"Are you sure you're doing this for the right reason, Rosie? I don't want to . . ."

She placed a finger over his lips. "Help me out. Please. I know you're a hard man in a fight but a gentleman in bed. And I've had my eye on you for quite some time."

Longarm could feel the heat and much more rising in his pants. "I've always felt an attraction to you, Rosie."

"I know that. A woman like me always knows when a

man is feeling something for her and that feeling is mutual. So how about it, lawman?"

Longarm was already tearing off his gun belt.

Rosie Red O'Brien had such long legs that she could wrap them around his waist and pull him deep inside. She laughed, squealed and did things that excited Longarm so bad that he took her four times before midnight. Took her from the front, top, bottom and from behind.

"You big galoot," she moaned. "I wish I'd have jumped you the first time you walked into this saloon. You've got a dong about three inches longer than Shake had and you know how to use it."

Longarm was half drunk by eleven o'clock and he felt as if he'd lost about ten pounds with all their wild coupling. Rosie, however, was insatiable. "How old are you?" he panted, pumping her like a bellows.

"Younger than you, big man." She twisted her head around to glance at him working hard and sweating profusely. "Are you fading on me?"

"Nope," Longarm said, pumping faster and harder. "I ain't fading at all."

"Good," she said, dropping her head down low to the bed. "'Cause I want you to make love to me all night long."

He came again and it felt like fire. "More brandy," Longarm gasped, flopping over on the bed. "And some water. I'm dryin' up."

"Water you shall have," she told him, climbing off the bed. "And food. You want food, don't you?"

"I could use something to eat so I can renew myself," he admitted. "Besides, I'm on my way to the Virginia City tomorrow morning on the stagecoach. Good damn thing I didn't rent a horse. I'd be too sore to mount the animal."

Rosie left the room for a minute and opened her door. She yelled something downstairs, and when she returned, announced, "Dinner is on its way. Hope you're hungry because I ordered something special."

"Oh, I sure as hell am."

Rosie poked him in the ribs. "You want to try it one more time? I've got an itch to show you a whole new position we could use."

"Later, please."

"What are you going up to Virginia City for?"

"I'm looking for Miss Lilly Claire."

"The singer and actress?"

"That's the one."

"Have you made love to her?"

Longarm was not a man to brag but he also hated liars. "I did have a dalliance with Lilly in Denver."

"Well," Rosie told him, "I'm not jealous or worried about losing you because Miss Claire just died."

Longarm's jaw dropped about three inches. "She what?"

"One of my customers just arrived from the Comstock Lode. He came in not fifteen minutes before I saw you in my saloon and told me that Miss Claire's body had been found below the balcony of her mountainside home. She had a bottle of whiskey in her hand and people in Virginia City think that she must have gotten drunk and fallen to her death."

Longarm jumped out of bed. "Is this news reliable?"

"Sure is. I didn't know Miss Claire, but I admired her talent. I've seen her on the street a number of times in Reno and she was so beautiful. Was she as good as I am in bed?"

He looked at Rosie and saw that she was serious and really wanted to know. "Nope. Not even close."

Longarm began to dress.

"Are you leaving me?"

He nodded. "Rosie I can't do anything more for you tonight."

"I understand. You really did care for Miss Claire."

"I suppose I did. As soon as I get up to Virginia City tomorrow, I'm going to be starting an investigation."

"On what?"

Longarm was buttoning his pants. "I'd be willing to bet everything I own that Lilly Claire's death was no accident. I'm betting she was murdered for her money."

Rosie nodded, her eyes sad and distant. "You know what? I think that Shake wanted to murder me for my money. I'm not sure I'd be alive today if he hadn't died while cheating at cards."

Longarm nodded but could think of nothing else to say.

Chapter 18

Virginia City, Nevada, was the Queen of the Comstock Lode. She had been born in the spring of 1859 when the forty-niners from California's played-out rivers and streams had stumbled upon a strange and sticky blue material that, when mixed with water, resembled crushed Concord grapes in flour. Those first miners had cussed at and tossed out the blue gooey mess until it was discovered that the strange material contained silver. Soon after that, the stampede was on as thousands of busted and idle miners had streamed over the Sierra Nevada mountains into the harsh high desert land where water was scarce and sagebrush plentiful.

The famous mining town on the steep slopes of Sun Mountain received its name when a drunken Irish miner named James "Old Virginny" Finney fell to the ground, broke his bottle of whiskey and used the last few drops of his liquor to christen the site Virginia City. Unlike many boom-and-bust mining towns the ore bodies hidden deep under Sun Mountain were monstrous but impossible for a man with a pick to reach, so the big mining companies arrived with heavy machinery transported by train and great ore wagons over the Sierras from Sacramento and San Francisco.

Soon, hundreds of thousands of miners were coming from all over the world to work the deep Comstock Lode mines hoping to get rich. The experienced hard-rock miners from Wales were especially in demand and a German fella whose name Longarm had forgotten created a brilliant system called "square set timbering" which allowed the miners to bore and tunnel a thousand feet into the steamy depths of the barren mountain. But despite the ingenious square set timbering, cave-ins and accidents killed hundreds of men; others were boiled alive when they sent picks into hidden pockets of hissing water. Through it all Virginia City continued to boom until the early 1880's when the great bodies of underground gold and silver were almost depleted.

Longarm knew all this because he had visited the Comstock Lode many times over the last decade and he was always impressed by the prosperity and the exuberance of the miners and store owners. In Virginia City, a man could be rich one day and broke the next because mining stocks fluctuated wildly as fortunes were made and lost overnight.

Now, as Longarm arrived at the steep and dangerous road that wound up from Washoe Valley he could see that Virginia City was in rapid decline, although he guessed there were still a few thousand citizens. In another five years, if history repeated itself as it had in a hundred other mining towns of the West, Longarm knew that Virginia City would be just another empty ghost town. Its magnificent Piper's Opera House and stately mansions once owned by silver kings were already falling into ruin.

Longarm wasted no time in visiting the marshal's office. But the man he had expected to find had quit and, in his place, was a hobbled old deputy who was probably paid a pittance from the town's shrinking coffers.

Longarm introduced himself to the old marshal and said, "I rushed up here to see the body of Miss Lilly Claire."

"Well," the marshal whose name was Hank Yary said, "you'll have to get in line. She's lyin' at rest over at O'Dell's Funeral Parlor and there's a lot of folks that want to pay their last respects to Miss Claire. You see, up here, she was one of our most famous and beloved citizens. Miss Claire helped fund the local hospital and our school. We've fallen on hard times, but she never gave up on us and was always generous. The folks here admire Miss Lilly Claire for much more than just her singing and stage talents. As far as people here are concerned she was a true saint who gave to every charity and every hard-luck miner who held out his hand for a little help."

"I didn't know that," Longarm said.

"Well, Miss Lilly never was one to make a fuss over herself. She built a mansion just two blocks up the hill and told everyone that she would stay here until the day that she died, just as our famous newspaper editor, Dan De-Quille has stayed even though we've fallen on hard times. 'Course Mr. DeQuille never had the fortune or fame of his contemporary, Mark Twain, but Old Dan is writing the history of this town. Gonna call his book *The Big Bonanza* and we're all hopin' it makes him even richer than Mark Twain who never came back to visit his friends."

Longarm was in a hurry and so he steered the conversation back to Lilly. "What do you know about Miss Claire's personal life?"

"Nothing at all," the marshal said. "Her business was never any of my business."

Longarm described Edward. "Was he really her brother?"

"Nope. Edward was her theatrical manager. Nobody understood why she kept him around. He is mean and unfriendly. He's also a leech, if you ask me. Him and his brother both."

"He had a *brother*?"

"Yep. Colonel Jack Hardy. And he's even meaner than his younger brother, Edward. 'Course, maybe that's because he saw so much blood spilled during his action in the Civil War. Even so, he's an arrogant one-armed son of a bitch, you ask me."

"*One armed?*" Longarm asked, suddenly all ears.

"Yep. Lost his left arm at Bull Run, or so he claims. He lived at Miss Claire's mansion claiming he was her bodyguard. But you know what I think?"

"No," Longarm said, "what do you think?"

"I think the colonel is just as worthless as his brother. I think they were both livin' off the bounty that Miss Lilly provided. And the reason that she didn't get rid of them Hardy brothers is that she was deathly afraid of 'em. Not that I blame her. They are dangerous and unpredictable men. When the town folks meet those Hardy boys on the street, they step into the dirt off the sidewalk just to let 'em pass."

"Have the Hardy brothers said anything about Miss Claire's death?"

"Now the colonel claims he was married to Miss Claire only the day before she died. Sounds damned fishy but he's got the marriage certificate in hand and he's suddenly acting like a grieving husband."

"I don't believe a word of it." Longarm spat in anger. "And I'll want to see that marriage document."

"Then you'll be the first to have the guts to ask to examine it," the old marshal said. "When it comes to the colonel, no one wants to question his truthfulness for fear of getting a lead bean in the belly."

"Including you, huh?"

The old deputy looked away and nodded sadly. "I know I should brace the colonel but I'm only paid twenty dollars a month and that sure ain't enough to die for."

"I understand."

Hank Yary seemed to be trying very hard to justify his inaction. "I got a wife and she ain't in good health," he continued as if he had not heard Longarm. "She's got the rheumatism real bad. Wants me to take her down to Yuma to live where the heat blazes all year around. But what would I do in Yuma?"

Longarm didn't answer because Deputy Yary already had his answer.

"I'd starve to death, that's what. Either that or be reduced to scrubbing out saloon spittoons or some other miserable job for pennies. At least here, I don't have to work too hard. And I do try to keep the peace. But not at the risk of my life. No sir! Not for twenty lousy dollars a month."

"You don't have to justify anything to me," Longarm said, realizing how guilty this man felt for not trying to get to the truth about Lilly's so-called accidental death. "I don't blame you for just trying to get by on so little pay and take care of your sick wife."

"Well, I *got* to do that," Yary said, still not meeting Longarm's eyes. "I bet you get paid three or four times what I get a month."

"I make considerably more money than you do. And that's why I'm going to take the risk and find out what really happened to Miss Claire."

"Don't see how you can do that," Yary said in a

crimped voice. "According to the Hardy men, Miss Claire just got stinkin' drunk and fell off the balcony."

"Wasn't there even a railing to protect someone from that kind of fatal mishap?"

"Oh yeah, there was a railing but poor Miss Claire busted right through it. Colonel Hardy says it was rotten and wasn't nailed properly. He says that it was just plain tragic and bad luck."

"I'll bet," Longarm said cryptically. "And now the colonel stands to gain a great deal of money."

"Well," Yary said. "There was a time maybe even just five years ago when this town was still in its bloomin' stage that Miss Claire's mansion was worth a fortune. But now that the mines are goin' broke, her mansion probably wouldn't bring more than five thousand dollars in this market. But things could turn around in a big hurry if more ore bodies are found way down under where we stand."

"And even if they aren't found," Longarm said, "the colonel and his brother stand to gain quite a lot of money. Five thousand here, another eight thousand there and who knows what Miss Claire had when you add the value of her jewelry, stocks and other assets."

"You're probably right," Yary agreed. "And now it'll all go to those two miserable sonsabitches."

"Not if I can prove that Edward and the colonel murdered Lilly."

"You really think that they did?"

"Don't you?"

"Yes, but, provin' it! Now that's the rub."

Longarm had heard enough. "I think I'll go take a close look at the body of Miss Claire and then I'll pay the Hardy brothers an official visit."

"Do you expect me to come along?" Yary asked, clearly worried.

"No. I'd rather do this alone."

Yary's relief was visible. "One of 'em will be there at O'Dell's Funeral Home. They take turns and ain't left Miss Lilly's side."

"When is the funeral?" Longarm asked.

"First thing tomorrow morning. A body, even that of a saint, don't last long in this heat."

Longarm headed for the door.

"Marshal?"

Longarm turned around. "Yeah?"

"Those brothers are quick on the trigger and handy with their knives. If you rile 'em, they'll come at you like the hounds of hell. Don't matter if you are a federal lawman. They'll drop you as fast as the beat of a humming-bird's wing."

"I'll keep that in mind," Longarm told the old man. "And I'll see you at the funeral tomorrow morning."

"Along with most of the town," Yary said. "We sure are gonna miss that lady real bad. Ain't nothin' good is happenin' on this ugly old Sun Mountain anymore. Businesses goin' under most every day. Mines closin' left and right. Been goin' downhill ever since Mark Twain went to California to write that damned jumpin' frog story that made him so famous. The city council is gonna have to let me go before long and I sure ain't lookin' forward to movin' down to Yuma."

"I understand," Longarm said with real sympathy. "It's all downhill for a lot of things these days. Just keep your head up and your powder dry, old-timer."

"And keep yourself alive," Yary called. "'Cause the minute you start askin' questions them Hardy boys are gonna consider you an enemy. And their enemies ain't long for this world."

Longarm supposed that was probably true. But deep inside, there was a cold, anvil-hard anger forming in his gut. He had cared deeply for Lilly, and now he was all but certain that two low-life bastards had pushed her over the edge of her balcony to her death. It was a sad, sick way to kill a famous as well as generous lady who was also considered a saint.

Longarm started marching down the boardwalk toward O'Dell's Funeral Parlor. He wasn't a bit eager to see Miss Lilly's remains most likely battered from her recent death plunge. The memory of their short but memorable hours together in Denver was still too fresh and Longarm knew that he would have to steel himself for this sad visit.

But he would do it for the great Lilly Claire and because the need for justice to be served was screaming in his heart.

Chapter 19

O'Dell's Funeral Parlor had once prospered. In the boom years it had taken good and reverent professional care of the final remains of the town's deceased at the rate of one per day. In the boom years the parlor had employed three full-time undertakers, one full-time casket maker and a stone carver. In these hard times, however, the funeral parlor was fortunate to handle one body a week and so the once-polished wooden floors were now dusty, the black hearse in the back shed that had been so impressive was falling into disrepair and the four matched white horses that once proudly pulled it up the main street were long since sold off. Nowadays Mr. O'Dell and his wife rented a set of mangy and mismatched mules to pull their hearse which they prayed would not break down before it reached the bleak and isolated cemetery located just a half mile east of town on a sun-blasted hill.

Longarm marched into the funeral parlor to see Edward Hardy sitting beside an empty casket, a half-empty bottle of whiskey in his hand. When the man looked up to see Longarm, he nearly dropped his bottle and jumped to his feet, blood draining from his handsome face.

"Hello, Edward," Longarm said pleasantly enough.

"What the hell are *you* doin' here?" Edward demanded.

"Paying my respects to Miss Lilly Claire just like everyone else in Virginia City."

"Her name is now Mrs. Lilly Hardy," Edward hissed. "She married my brother before she had her accident."

"So I've learned."

"Well, if you know that then I suggest you go outside and wait like everyone else. This is *family* business."

"Is that what you call it?" Longarm asked, a cold, cutting hardness rising in his voice. "You consider yourself family because your brother claims to have married Lilly Claire only a day before she fell to her death? What an amazing misfortune . . . or good fortune, if you are guilty of murder."

Edward paled. He swallowed hard and said, "I didn't like you when you were in Denver and I damn sure don't like you any better now. Lilly didn't need you for protection because she had me."

"Either way," Longarm said, "she's dead. Maybe we both failed her."

"Get out of here!"

Longarm walked right up to the man and jabbed a forefinger in his chest. "Do you care to tell me how she's getting buried a *second* time?"

Edward took a back step, his eyes burning with unbridled hatred. "I don't know what the hell you are talking about, Marshal Long."

"I'm talking about Lilly supposedly getting shot to death when I went to meet her in a Denver park. Only the woman who was buried at the Eternal Rest Cemetery was *not* Lilly. No, it was a stranger. Some poor unknown woman placed in a casket and meant to dupe everyone into thinking Lilly was dead when she really was not."

The man wiped his face and sucked in some deep breaths. Longarm could see sweat beading on Edward's brow. The man finally blurted, "Marshal Long, you must be drunker'n I am."

Longarm shook his head. "Where is Lilly's body?"

He pointed. "It's in the other room. But you keep away from her. She was my sister."

"Sister?" Longarm snorted with derision. "Yeah, that's what you said she was in Denver. But now that the colonel has married her, she's also your ex–sister-in-law. Isn't that right?"

Edward was either too drunk to stay with Longarm mentally or too stupid, it really didn't matter. "You just . . . just keep away from her," he warned. "You've got no business being here. You didn't mean anything to her."

"I was hired to offer protection . . . which I'm ashamed to say I failed to adequately provide." Longarm started past Edward, warning, "I've got a lot of questions to ask you, mister."

He went through the only doorway in the room and found himself in a large embalming area. Miss Lilly was wrapped up in cool wet cloths in an attempt to keep her body from decomposing in the stifling heat. Once, the funeral parlor had used ice hauled down from the highest Sierra Nevada peaks, but now that was far too expensive.

A middle-aged couple burst into the room. The man was small and unhealthy looking with thick spectacles and a prominent hooked nose. His wife was equally unattractive, heavy and frowning. It was she who said, "Who are you and what are you doing here?"

Longarm produced his badge. "I'm here to investigate the suspicious circumstances of Miss Claire's death."

"Her name was changed to Mrs. Hardy." She placed

her hands on her wide hips. "You have no authority to intrude on us at this time. We are trying to prepare for tomorrow morning's funeral."

Longarm ignored the fat woman and went over to gaze down at Miss Lilly Claire. Her face was terribly swollen, blue and battered. If he hadn't known Lilly before, he might not have recognized her now. The corpse was perfumed but still an oppressive odor of death made him want to flee the room.

"Don't you dare touch her!" the fat woman cried. "Can't you show at least a little respect for the dead!"

Because the woman was so overbearing, Longarm turned to Mr. O'Dell. "Sir, I'd like you both to leave the room. Do it now before I lose patience."

O'Dell took his wife's arm. She shrugged off his grip and came at Longarm. "You have no right to be here! Now you must leave at once or I will send for the colonel."

"Why don't you go and do that?" Longarm suggested. "It would save me hunting the son of a bitch down."

The woman's nostrils flared and she made a noise like a teased sow. Before she could say anything more, her husband somehow managed to pull her out of the room leaving Longarm alone with Lilly's corpse.

His examination was quick, but thorough. The body was decomposing at an alarming rate yet he had to see if there were any physical marks of violence that he could identify apart from what would be expected from a fatal fall.

"The neck," he said out loud to himself, staring at it. "Bruises that couldn't have come from a long fall, even if her neck were broken on impact."

Longarm could almost trace the finger marks that had dug into Lilly's once beautiful flesh. "No doubt she was grabbed around the neck. Probably just before being shoved off the balcony."

He forced himself to unwrap the body and examine it from head to toe. It was one of the worst things he'd done in many years. The full-body examination took less than three minutes, and when Longarm was done, he felt as if he wanted to vomit and then kill the Hardy brothers. But he couldn't do that because he still had no real proof that they were behind this terrible murder.

So how could he prove that Lilly had been murdered? Well, she did have severe bruises around her throat and unmistakable finger marks that even a half-blind man would not fail to notice.

The answer suddenly became clear to Longarm: he would have to force or trick one or both of the Hardy men to confess to the murder.

Longarm rewrapped the body, turned aside and lit a cigar. He inhaled deeply, trying to drive off the nearly overpowering stench of death. Then he pivoted around and touched Lilly's pale lips with his fingertips whispering, "I'll bring them down. I'm just sorry I let you down in Denver. I'll always be sorry for that. Good-bye and may your soul already have winged its way to heaven."

The outer parlor was empty now except for the open casket that would hold Lilly early tomorrow morning before being loaded onto the hearse for Miss Claire's final, public journey.

Longarm checked his hideout derringer and sidearm, then took the chair that Edward had vacated and smoked thoughtfully. He knew with complete certainty that both the Hardy men would soon come bursting into this funeral home and they would be loaded for bear and ready to do battle.

Well and good. It would be easier ... much easier ... simply to try his best to kill them rather than to attempt to get them to confess to their heinous murder for money. They would *never* confess, he was certain of that. And unless there was a witness that he did not know about to the murder Longarm knew that killing Edward and the colonel would be his only option when it came to meting out pure, unfettered frontier justice.

Slow minutes passed. Longarm noticed a crowd outside the funeral parlor gathering to see what would happen. He was sure that the word was out that a federal marshal had come all the way from Colorado to visit Miss Lilly Claire and investigate the unlikely circumstances surrounding her death.

Longarm stood up and moved his chair farther from the front window so that he could not be easily seen by the gathering crowd. He wondered if the colonel was stupid enough to come in with guns blazing.

Probably not. Even way out here on the Comstock Lode where there was little law except that of the gun, shooting down a federal officer with a crowd watching was begging to be arrested, tried and hanged. No, the colonel and Edward would have to be more circumspect. More devious. So what would the Hardy brothers do or say?

Longarm laid his double-action Colt .44–40 in his lap and waited for what he was sure would be their sudden and dramatic entrance with anticipation.

Chapter 20

Longarm didn't have to wait very long. In less time than it took for him to finish his cigar, the Hardy brothers came bursting into the funeral parlor. The colonel was in the lead and he was shaking with unconcealed fury.

"I heard what you said to my brother."

"Oh," Longarm said, not rising from his chair or bothering to holster his gun. "I said several things to Edward. Which ones are you referring to?"

"You implied that my wife was *murdered*!"

"Yeah, I did," Longarm said. "And I also implied that you and Edward are the murderers."

The colonel was wearing a sidearm and he started to make a play but Longarm had his own gun up and trained on the enraged man's chest before he could draw iron.

Longarm's lips formed into a cold grin. "Colonel, go ahead and draw that pistol of yours because I'd like to close this case *right now*. And Edward, why don't you go for your gun, too? That would really wrap this up for me and I could go home to Denver with a clear conscience that justice has been served."

Edward's eyes widened and he took a step back. He glanced at his older brother and whispered, "Don't do it, Jack. He'll kill us both!"

The colonel must have seen that this was exactly what the outcome would be if he pulled his gun up even an inch. With great effort, the one-armed man inhaled, then exhaled and slowly raised his hands away from his weapon.

"You're going to pay for that accusation, Marshal. I'm going to find out who your superior is and I'll make sure that you are jailed or even imprisoned for slandering an American war hero."

If the situation hadn't been so tense, Longarm would have laughed out loud.

"I fought in the war, too, colonel. But I don't go around reminding people of it. And one thing I learned is that any man who beats or kills a woman or child is the lowest kind of son of a bitch on earth. Guess where that places you in my mind?"

Longarm's words were meant to provoke the colonel into making a play for his gun so that he could be killed. And, if Edward also lost his mind and went to his pistol, that would be icing on the cake.

"Gawdamn you!" the colonel shouted, starting to draw.

"No!" Edward protested, grabbing his older brother's arm and pinning it to his side. "Don't you see that the marshal wants us to draw so he can kill us?"

The colonel's struggle was brief, possibly even staged in order to salvage the last visage of his dignity. He backed out the door. "I don't want to ever see you again, Marshal. And you'd damn sure better not be at my wife's funeral tomorrow morning. If you are, I'll gun you down like a damned dog."

Longarm could have arrested the man right on the spot for threatening the life of a federal law officer. But he let the warning pass because he wanted to take the colonel down for murder.

"I'll be there. And after the funeral, I'll want to see that marriage certificate as well as the preacher who married you. He and I will have some words."

"What?" the colonel screamed.

"You heard me," Longarm said. "The certificate and the preacher. I'll want to see both tomorrow morning."

The colonel started to curse but Edward dragged his enraged brother out the door saving his life.

The undertaker and his wife had been listening and now they emerged from the embalming room. "You git out of here!" the fat woman shouted. "You got no right to accuse those men of murder."

"Sure I do," Longarm said. "I can accuse them of whatever I want. All I need now is a little more proof."

"You have no proof at all!" Mrs. O'Dell ranted.

Longarm was brutally blunt. "And I suppose those finger bruise marks on Miss Claire's throat were caused when someone lifted her up by the neck *after* she was dead?"

Mrs. O'Dell started to say something and then stopped as if a chicken bone had suddenly lodged in her throat. It was clear that Longarm's observation and resulting question had caught her by surprise. With no response possible, the woman whirled around and vanished.

"What about you, Mr. O'Dell? Don't tell me you didn't see those marks that are the classic sign of strangulation. My bet is that the poor woman was dead before she was thrown through the balcony railing."

O'Dell didn't say a word.

"Yeah," Longarm told him. "I can see that you know I'm right. But I also see that you're as scared of the Hardy brothers as everyone else in this town seems to be."

173

O'Dell suddenly looked terribly ashamed.

Longarm pressed even harder. "Who is it that supposedly married Miss Claire and Colonel Jack Hardy?"

"Please, I . . ."

"Dammit, answer me!"

"Preacher Winfield. Hosea Winfield," the undertaker croaked.

"Does he have a church?"

"Yes."

"Where is it?" Longarm asked. "I'm going to see him right now."

"But I heard you say to the colonel that you were going to talk to him after the service tomorrow morning."

"I lied," Longarm admitted. "Now tell me where I can find this preacher man."

"His church is the Bucket of Blood Saloon. Preacher Winfield not only finds solace in the Bible, but I'm afraid he also finds it in a whiskey bottle."

Longarm knew where the Bucket of Blood was located. In fact, it was one of his favorite watering holes with a spectacular view of the eastern panorama of undulating rocks, sage and hills.

"Thanks, O'Dell. And one more thing."

The man finally met his eyes. "What's that?"

"Put her in the casket and keep it closed. Lilly wouldn't have liked anyone to see her looking the way she does now."

"I understand you perfectly."

"Good," Longarm said, turning for the door. "Oh, one other thing?"

O'Dell nodded. "Yes?"

"If I were you I wouldn't tell the Hardy brothers that I went to see Preacher Winfield. Do you understand me?"

"I most certainly do."

Longarm had a sudden thought and dug into his pocket. He brought out five dollars and handed it to the shaken undertaker. "Buy some flowers and put them in her hair."

"But no one will see them in a closed-casket funeral."

"It doesn't matter," Longarm said, knowing he was making no sense. "Lilly Claire was beautiful and there should be flowers with her when she is covered by earth."

"Yes, sir."

Having nothing more to say, Longarm went to find the alcoholic preacher to determine if he had actually married Lilly and the colonel or if he even had the authority to do so.

The Reverend Hosea Winfield had once been a Methodist minister whose future in San Francisco had been most promising during the height of the forty-niner Gold Rush. He had the gift and power of words and had been fiercely passionate about doing God's work. But a series of personal tragedies and the long years of time had broken the man and now, when Longarm found him in the Bucket of Blood Saloon, the man was but a shell of his former self.

Winfield was holding a bottle of rotgut whiskey by the huge bay window that looked east out past the wind-whipped cemetery where Lilly would soon lie. He was a tall man, bent and stooped more by his sorrows than by his hard and tragic years.

"Reverend," Longarm said after the bartender had pointed out the solitary man, "I am . . ."

"I know who you are and I know what you're going to ask me," the reverend said. "But I can't tell you anything."

Longarm had purchased a mug of beer at the bar and now he took a seat at Winfield's table beside the huge window even though he was uninvited. "You *have* to tell me, Reverend. Too much depends on the answers you must provide."

The man looked up. His eyes were red and swollen causing Longarm to wonder if it was from drink or from crying over the death of Lilly. Perhaps it was a lot of both.

Winfield seemed to look through Longarm as he said, "If I tell you the truth, my life is over on this earth."

"Meaning the Hardy brothers will kill you?"

"Exactly so. And, to be honest, it would probably be a mercy. I've lived too long in the darkness of shadows. It is time to meet my Judgment Day and that is what I fear the most."

"We all fear that day. Meet it bravely and tell me what I must know," Longarm said, refilling the reverend's glass.

The man had great unsightly bags under his eyes. His hair was black, streaked with silver and his flesh was loose and colorless. To Longarm, it appeared as if the reverend were merely a ghost waiting to pass into an uncertain eternity.

"Are you an ordained preacher?" Longarm asked, deciding not to wait any longer for an answer.

"Yes, I am."

"So you have the authority to legally perform marriages?"

Winfield smiled and it was heartbreaking. "Not anymore. Not really."

"Meaning?"

"I was excommunicated from my church many years ago."

"For what reason?"

"That is between me and God. I have already confessed my damning sins to those with the power to absolve them. I will not confess them again to you."

Longarm could tell that the man was not going to be swayed from that decision and it probably wasn't a relevant question anyway. "All right. So why did you perform the marriage between the colonel and Miss Claire?"

"For money. And because I had no real choice."

"You were threatened?"

He nodded and tapped his bottle on their scarred little table. "And bribed handsomely."

"Did Miss Claire marry the colonel of her own free will?"

"I doubt it. I believe she was totally incapacitated by opium."

"What makes you think that?"

"I could smell it on her and she had that look in her eyes that the opium fiends possess. You've seen it as often as I."

"Yes," Longarm said, "I have. So, if she was incapacitated and coerced into this marriage, why did you perform it?"

"I already told you. I was bribed and threatened."

"The marriage is worthless. It wouldn't stand up in a court of law."

"No," Winfield whispered. "Most certainly not. But Miss Claire is dead. So how can she testify that it was an invalid marriage?"

"She can't and doesn't need to. All you have to do is accompany me to a judge and swear to him that you are no longer authorized to perform a valid marriage ceremony."

"If I do that . . ."

"You *will* do it," Longarm vowed. "It's the very least you can do for Miss Claire."

The man was silent so long that Longarm wondered if he had gone into a trance. Finally, he said, "Yes. I suppose it is."

Winfield held his bottle up to the big window next to

him and studied it thoughtfully. "This bottle is empty. An empty vessel like myself."

"Men have lost their souls and found them again. Preachers, too. You can start over."

"No," he said quietly, "because there is nothing good left in me. Only sickness and sorrow. Will you buy me another bottle for courage and hope?"

Longarm paused. "All right. But tomorrow we'll find a judge and right a wrong."

"Whatever you say, Marshal."

Longarm got up feeling empty and depressed. He had seen many men who had fallen into despair, but it was always somehow more deeply affecting when it was a former man of the cloth. A man of intellect and a once-great promise.

He went to the bar and said, "Another bottle for the Reverend Winfield. Whatever it is that he's drinking."

"The cheapest whiskey we sell," the bartender said, shaking his head. "He doesn't care anymore. He doesn't even taste the stuff."

"Just bring the bottle," Longarm told the man as he turned to go back to join the preacher.

Suddenly, a bullet shattered the huge plate glass window. Then another. And before Longarm could reach Winfield, the man's skull hit the table and his blood began to form a dark halo around the hole blasted through his brain.

Chapter 21

The murder of Reverend Winfield had been a shock and it happened so suddenly that Longarm knew that he might have been shot as well had he not gone for a replacement bottle of bad whiskey. His gun came to his hand and he saw the colonel and Edward down on the mountainside scrambling to conceal themselves. To get a clean shot, they'd had to venture onto exposed ground and abandon concealment.

"I'm coming for you!" Longarm shouted, unleashing two bullets on the men just as they disappeared behind a mine's tailings.

Longarm ran over to the bar. "I need a rifle."

The bartender backed away, throwing his hands in the air. "I don't want any part of . . ."

"Dammit, give me a rifle! I know you have one back there."

Up came a double-barreled shotgun. Longarm would have preferred a Winchester but the shotgun and his pistol would have to do the job. He tore the shotgun out of the bartender's sweaty hands and checked to make sure that it was loaded.

"Give me some extra shells!"

The bartender spilled a half dozen shells across the top of the polished bar. Longarm jammed them into his coat pocket and took off running out the door. He ran around a building and down toward the V&T Railroad Depot which was abandoned when the mines shut down.

The Hardy brothers were armed with repeating rifles putting Longarm at a severe disadvantage. He needed to shorten the firing range and he needed to do it quick.

Longarm was accustomed to high altitude and was in excellent shape. Better shape, it soon became apparent, than the pair of ruthless and cunning murderers he now pursued. They ran and fired on the run, ducking behind old rusty mining machinery and deserted boxcars and locomotives. Longarm was relentless and determined. He stayed low, moved fast and only fired to keep the brothers off balance. At last, he saw them disappear into the opening of the Sutro Mine Tunnel. It had been dug to drain the boiling waters from the deepest mines but had proved to be too late and too little to show a profit. Now, it was simply a gaping hole in the earth.

Longarm cautiously entered the tunnel which ran for a good eight miles down to the lower desert. But he knew that the men he chased weren't going to run nearly that far. No, they'd be waiting to ambush him and they'd stay close to the mouth of the tunnel.

Longarm paused to catch his breath and listen. He heard no thudding of footsteps. No hard breathing. Nothing at all.

"Come out and surrender. You are both under arrest for murder."

The colonel screamed. "Come and get us, Marshal. We're waiting!"

Longarm realized that even though he was outnumbered, the shotgun now gave him a slight advantage.

"Who was that dead woman you substituted for Lilly in Denver?"

"She was a whore. A nobody. She got a great funeral instead of being buried in a pauper's grave."

"Why did you do it?"

"We needed to get Lilly away from you and everyone else!"

"Damn you both," Longarm yelled. "The Reverend Winfield told me that you drugged Lilly with opium. That means the marriage means nothing!"

"The reverend is dead!"

Longarm heard the colonel's sick laughter and he shouted, "Surrender. This is your last chance!"

"Come and get us, Marshal and we'll send you on your way straight to hell!"

Longarm tiptoed up to a corner of the tunnel. He was still close enough to the wide mouth of the Sutro so that there was a faint light. He decided that it would be suicide to go farther.

"I'll wait you bastards out no matter how long it takes."

"Come and get us!"

Longarm took a deep breath and considered the situation carefully. He would be silhouetted against the light if he stepped around the corner and that was when they would open a deadly fire. He knew that he could not step out and be a lighted target and expect to survive.

So what to do next?

He had an inspiration. Longarm backed out of the tunnel and retreated down the train tracks knowing that the brothers would not try to escape believing that he was still hidden and waiting in the tunnel. Longarm ran until he found a small, independent mine still operating and quickly told the miner his needs.

"Dynamite," he shouted. "Two sticks ought to do it. Hurry!"

He got the two sticks and even paid the miner. Then he went back to the mouth of the Sutro and lit one of the sticks. He hurled it into the tunnel and jumped behind a rusty ore cart.

The explosion was deafening and it collapsed the mouth of the tunnel except for a few feet of opening at the top. Longarm lit the second stick of dynamite and hurled it up on the pile of newly fallen rocks half shrouded in a cloud of swirling dust.

Bam! The earth shook under his feet and the tunnel was gone!

Longarm stood up and proudly surveyed his handiwork. Satisfied, he walked back to the miner and said, "Those sticks of dynamite worked just fine. I'll buy two more."

The miner couldn't seem to tear his eyes away from the cloud of dust and what had been the famous Sutro Mine Tunnel. "My god, are you buryin' the Hardy brothers *alive?*"

"That's up to them," Longarm replied. "Is the lower mouth of the tunnel still open?"

"Sure but it's miles down this mountainside!"

"Yeah," Longarm said with a smile. "The colonel and his murdering brother are going to have a hell of a tough time getting to the other opening."

"They sure will."

"And I'll be waiting," Longarm vowed.

• • •

He was waiting many hours later when the brothers staggered out into sunlight far below Virginia City. They were covered with dirt and wet grime, squinting and staggering like drunks on a midday binge.

"Hands up!" Longarm shouted from atop his rented horse.

The Hardy men still clutched their guns in their dirty fists, which was a huge mistake. Almost as great a mistake as when they raised their pistols, squinted into the blinding light of day and tried to open fire at the blurred shape of a vengeful horseman.

Longarm shot them to pieces with both barrels of his shotgun. The colonel and Edward were torn apart and hurled back into the lower mouth of the empty Sutro Tunnel.

Then, Longarm reined in the horse he'd confiscated and rode slowly back up to Virginia City in the fading light of day.

He had an important funeral to attend in the morning, when he planned to commune with the spirit of the late and lovely Miss Lilly Claire. He'd tell Lilly that justice had finally been served. That her mansion and all her wealth would not fall into the bloody hands of murderers but instead would go toward her favorite Comstock charities.

Longarm liked that idea, and for the first time in quite a while, he felt good inside and well pleased with himself. On his way back up Sun Mountain, he also thought about Miss Sara Lancaster waiting for him in his Denver apartment. She'd probably domesticated the place and ruined it completely.

That was okay with Longarm. He and his cat Midnight would enjoy getting Sara straightened. It would be two mangy males against one pretty female. And a reasonable man could hope for no better odds.

Watch for

LONGARM AND THE SCARLET RIDER

the 323rd novel in the exciting LONGARM series
from Jove

Coming in October!

**Explore the exciting Old West with one
of the men who made it wild!**

LONGARM

AND THE DEADLY DEAD MAN

IN THIS GIANT-SIZED ADVENTURE,
AN OUTLAW LEARNS THAT HE'S
SAFER IN HIS GRAVE THAN
FACING AN AVENGING ANGEL
NAMED LONGARM.

0-515-13547-X

J. R. ROBERTS
THE GUNSMITH